Night of Secrets

NIGHT OF SECRETS

COURT OF MIDSUMMER MAYHEM

BOOK 2

TARA GRAYCE

NIGHT OF SECRETS

LCCN: 2023914755

ISBN: 978-1-943442-47-8

N
W
E
S
Court of Ice
Wilderness Court
Court of Artisans
Goblin Court
Court of Stone
Court of Mists
Court of Islands
Harvest Court
Court of Sand
Melrena
Court of Sand
Court of Grass
Court of Revels
Great Library
Tanglewood
King Oberon & Queen Titania's Court
Queen Mab's Court
Court of Knowledge
Court of Dreams
Court of Jungles
Court of Seas
Queen Hippolyta's Court
Swamp Court
Court of Swordmaidens
Fae Realm

Chapter One

The last time Viola stepped through a door into the unknown, she had been on the back of a talking pony being either kidnapped or rescued by her sister's fae husband, depending on how one looked at it.

Rescued was the more accurate description, though there was a little snatching thrown in there, thanks to the Laws of Bindings that governed the Fae Realm.

Standing in the middle of her bedroom in the House that had been her home for the past seven years, Viola smoothed her hands over her dark gray skirt, white shirt, and green librarian coat, which signified that she had risen to the job of assistant librarian in the Great Library. After checking the magical pockets of the coat for librarian supplies, she stuck her hand into the magical pocket of her skirt, rifling through the few belongings she had accumulated in her family's seven years here in the Fae Realm.

Her entire life was compressed into a single pocket. Granted, it was a magical pocket that could fit far more on the inside than it appeared. But something still ached in her chest at the thought.

Around her, the House gave a huffy shudder, raining dirt on her.

"Yes, yes, I know. I need to get moving." Viola patted the nearest wall. Years ago, it would have been strange to talk to a house. Now, it was just normal life.

Despite her words, Viola stared at the Anywhere Door that led from her bedroom to the rest of the House, unable to force her feet to move.

When they had left the Human Realm, her entire family had stepped into a new life together, fleeing the dangers of the drought and a man who intended to sell them into indentured servitude.

This time, Viola would step into a new life with only her brother Sebastian at her side. The rest of her family was staying here in the Court of Knowledge, continuing their lives without them.

"I'm not sure if I'm ready to go." Viola dug her fingers into the moss that clung to the walls. One of the flowering vines hanging from the ceiling twitched, then patted her hand, as if the House was offering comfort.

Would this room disappear once she left? The House had added the rooms to the Anywhere Door when Viola and her siblings had moved in. Would the room simply disappear back to the magical limbo as soon as it was no longer needed?

Viola clenched her fists and drew in a deep breath, trying to banish the lump clogging her throat at the thought of her room simply vanishing into the void. She blinked rapidly, unable to force herself to say the final goodbye to this room.

She didn't want to leave. Her home was here. With her family and their talking pony companion Buddy and the Great Library and everything that had become so familiar the past seven years.

But she didn't want her brother Sebastian to miss this opportunity either. After nearly two years of negotiating, Sebastian had finally convinced Duke Orsino, a ruling lord of one of the isles in the Court of Islands, to build an outpost library. Sebastian and Viola were going to run it.

She and Sebastian had always done everything together. While their two older sisters Meg and Brigid were busy providing for and protecting the family, Viola and Sebastian had looked after each other, and together took care of Beatrice, their youngest sibling. If Viola said she wasn't going, then Sebastian wouldn't either.

She couldn't hold him back. This outpost library had been his primary goal for the past two years. She had never seen Sebastian so set on anything in his life, except perhaps learning sword fighting when they first moved to the Fae Realm.

The flowering vine stopped patting her arm, and the House gave another shudder around her. The floor lifted up, the vines shoving against her back, as the House all but thrust her at the door.

Well, the House was making her decision for her. It was time to step through the door and face the day.

After one last look at the room that had been hers for the past seven years—the first room she'd ever had to herself—she stepped through the Anywhere Door into the main room of the House.

The rest of the family gathered around the crowded table that filled most of the space. Basil and Meg claimed the end of the table with their two girls in their chairs to either side of them. Beatrice squeezed in next to them while Sebastian sat across from her. Even Brigid and Munch had come over from their House next door and crowded in at the foot of the table.

They were all talking and laughing so loudly that Viola couldn't make out any of the conversations, nor had anyone even noticed that she had entered the room.

Buddy, their talking pony companion, stuck his head over the half door that separated his stable from the main part of the House. He regarded her family with a baleful look in his deep brown eyes.

Viola eased around the perimeter of the room until she stood next to Buddy. She ran her fingers over his soft, brown hair, digging her fingers into the coarse strands of his thick mane.

Buddy eyed her, giving a soft snort through his large nostrils. "An obnoxiously boisterous bunch, aren't they? I haven't had a decent morning's sleep since you all moved in."

"But you love us anyway." Viola drew in a deep breath of his musk and grass horse smell. There was just something so comforting and warm about leaning against the pony.

Buddy just snorted, but the twinkle in his eyes gave him away. He nipped the hem of her librarian coat with his large, blunt teeth, giving a tug. "Don't forget about us when you leave for that shiny, warm island of yours and Sebastian's."

Viola swallowed back the choking lump in her throat. "I could never forget you. Or the Court of Knowledge. Or anyone here."

"None of that now. You know I'm a sympathetic crier." Buddy nudged her with his nose.

"You're a pony. You can't cry. Well, I suppose you could. Ponies do have tear glands. You just don't use tears as an emotional release like humans and fae." Viola snapped her mouth shut. Could she make it more obvious that, once Basil had taught her to read, she had become a little obsessive, reading through as much of the Great Library as she could?

Which wasn't as impressive as it sounded. The Great Library was massive. She'd barely put a dent in the knowledge still to be learned.

"My point exactly." Buddy nipped the hem of her coat again. "You're still a librarian. You're still a citizen of the Court of Knowledge. You're still a part of this family. You're just going to be galloping to new horizons, so to speak. Every foal needs to, eventually."

Viola briefly leaned her head against Buddy's neck, drawing in his warmth and steadiness. What was she going to do in the Court of Islands without a talking pony companion to talk sense into her?

Spread her wings. Or gallop to the horizon. Whatever metaphor or colloquialism one wanted to use.

"You'll be able to pop back through the Anywhere Doors anytime. As will we. You won't be able to get rid of us that easily." Buddy curved his neck and nudged her with his nose again, pushing her toward the table. "Now sit down with your family and eat your breakfast. It isn't wise to step into an adventure on an empty stomach."

"Thanks, Buddy." Viola glanced over her shoulder, then let her momentum carry her toward the table where a single empty chair waited for her. She slipped into it, reaching for a plate piled high with her favorite pink toast. Several kinds of jelly—in colors from fuchsia to vermilion—sat in pots on the table.

"Are you ready to take the leap through the Door today?" Brigid leaned forward and grinned at Viola, then at Sebastian.

Sebastian grinned right back. "I've been counting down to today for months now."

"Me too." Viola hoped her smile hid any lingering trepidation.

"We will miss having you here." Meg reached out and wiped a smear of jelly from Addy's face as the four-year-old squirmed. "Especially your help with the girls. You volunteer to watch them so often. I'm not sure what we will do without you."

"You'll still have me." Beatrice dumped more fruit onto Morgan's plate, earning a grin from the two-year-old. "I don't mind watching them."

"I know, but I don't want to ask you too much." Meg shared a glance with Basil. "At least the Library is a great help."

Viola forced herself to eat her toast, despite the churning in her stomach. Almost, she wanted to call the whole thing off. Just tell everyone she was staying here. They wouldn't judge her. She would always have a home here and a place at the Great Library.

But if she did that, Sebastian would be on his own. Or he wouldn't go at all.

All too soon, breakfast was over, and Viola found herself swept up into hugs and farewells. Her family was doing this here in the House where they had privacy. Once they stepped into the Hall of Anywhere Doors, they would be surrounded by others.

As Sebastian hugged their nieces, Brigid tugged Viola aside. "I have something for you." She held out a necklace formed of a clear, woven string with an amber pendant featuring a small, purple flower encased inside.

Viola's eyes widened as she reached out and took the necklace. "Isn't this one of the glamour necklaces the pixies gave you? Don't you need it for your…work?"

Viola didn't know much about what her sister did as the Wild Fae Primrose, beyond that she *was* the Primrose. That hero who rescued kidnapped people—whether they were humans snatched by the fae or fae stolen by humans. Even that much knowledge was dangerous, and Brigid couldn't tell Viola more than that.

Brigid nodded. "Yes, but the pixies were generous. I have more than enough of the glamour necklaces for my uses. I'd like you to have one, just in case."

Viola curled her fingers over the necklace, her heart thumping harder. "Do you think we will be in danger?"

"I haven't heard anything specific regarding the Court of Islands." Brigid's mouth twisted a bit, that humor she wore as a cloak fading as she met Viola's eyes. "But it's an unsettled time for the courts right now, and the Court of Islands doesn't have a single, uniting king or queen the way the rest of the Courts do. Sebastian has trained with a sword, but you don't have a way to defend yourself. This necklace could give you a chance, if you run into trouble."

Viola swallowed and gripped the necklace tighter in her fingers. She wasn't the fighter that Sebastian was. She didn't have Brigid's head for wiggling out of trouble or Meg's spunk. At times, the Court of Knowledge felt so safe—or as relatively safe as anywhere in the Fae Realm ever could be—

that Viola hadn't felt the need to learn any sort of self-defense besides the basics that all librarians learned. She had her club, the one she used to fight monsters when the Library was attacked, but that was it.

Fighting monsters was one thing. Fighting a fae was another.

"Wear this necklace at all times." Brigid gestured to Viola, then the necklace she held. "When you want to use the glamour, hold it in your hand, envision how you wish to appear, then put the necklace under your bodice against your skin. When you want to end the glamour, take the necklace back out so that the pendant is no longer touching your skin."

That seemed simple enough.

"The glamour will make whoever is looking at you see and hear the person they think you are." Brigid's grin took on a wry twist. "But the glamour isn't as strong as the glamour a fae can put on themselves. If someone touches you, they will be able to see beneath the glamour. Someone who knows either you or the person you are pretending to be very well will start to see beneath it, though the closer you are to the person you are pretending to be, the harder it will be to see beneath the glamour. It isn't perfect, but it gets the job done in a pinch."

Viola nodded and clasped the necklace around her neck, letting the amber pendant fall onto her white shirt. "Thank you. Hopefully I won't need it, but I will keep it close."

"You and Sebastian will be just fine, I'm sure." Brigid hugged Viola, then stepped back. "I'll drop by when I can, though I haven't had reason to step on Duke Orsino's island before. That's a mark in his favor."

It was. If Brigid didn't need to visit that particular island, then Duke Orsino and his people weren't in the habit of stealing humans.

Sebastian had said he had been treated well on his visits in the past two years. He wouldn't be so excited about this move if Duke Orsino had proven to be less than hospitable toward humans. Nor would King Theseus have agreed to such an alliance with Duke Orsino's island if he hadn't been at least somewhat trustworthy.

All too soon, the farewells were finished, and they trooped through the Anywhere Door, stepping into the Hall of Anywhere Doors connecting King Theseus's palace and the Great Library.

White marble floors spread out before them, flowing into the marble walls. Pillars shaped like gnarled trees lined the grand space while a ceiling formed of broad skylights arched overhead. Between the pillars, the two long sides of the hall contained long rows of Anywhere Doors, connecting the Great Library with its many outpost libraries and with every Court of the Fae Realm. Even at this time of morning, fae of all shapes, sizes, and colors bustled in and out of the Anywhere Doors, then headed for the double doors on the far end that led to the Great Library, seeking answers to their questions or to pick out a new book.

To one side of the Hall of Anywhere Doors, King Theseus and Queen Hippolyta stood, the regal librarian king and his warrior queen. King Theseus's black, short-cropped hair contrasted with Queen Hippolyta's golden curls. While he wore a black coat trimmed in gold, she dressed in a simple white dress layered with chainmail.

Beside them, Head Librarian Marco stood several inches shorter than either the king or queen. His white beard flowed nearly to his knees while his head had only wisps of hair. He held a large basket in both arms.

With a glance at Viola, Sebastian marched forward and bowed to King Theseus and Queen Hippolyta. "I am honored that you have entrusted me to head this new outpost library."

"It has been your idea from the beginning. I am pleased to see it coming to fruition." King Theseus nodded, a smile creasing his angular features. "Librarian Sebastian, Librarian Viola, may you bring the light of knowledge to this new corner of the Fae Realm."

Viola stepped forward and curtsied to her fae king and queen. "We will, Your Majesties."

Head Librarian Marco smiled warmly as he held out the basket to Viola. "I know that both of you will do well. Viola, I trust you will take good care of this."

She took the basket, then peered inside.

A tiny sapling rested inside, its root ball wrapped in burlap and tied off with twine. Around it, four blue bookwyrms curled, their scaled and legless bodies protecting this piece of the Great Library's tree.

Viola hugged the basket to her chest, then scratched each of the bookwyrms behind their ruffs in turn. "Hello, Curio. Toby. Belch. Feste. I'm honored that you chose to go with us to the outpost library."

Curio, the largest of the bookwyrms, nuzzled her hand, his scales rasping against her skin. She laughed and gave him an extra scratch.

She and Sebastian would need to plant this tree in the light of the full moon, which fell on the twelfth night after their arrival in the Court of Islands. On that night, it would sprout and turn the outpost library into a living extension of the Great Library.

Still hugging the basket to her, Viola turned to take in her family one more time.

Basil had an arm around Meg's shoulder. His black, master librarian coat was as pristine as ever, matching his slightly tousled dark brown hair. He had been Viola's first brother-in-law, and he had been the one who had rescued all of them from the Human Realm so many years ago.

Meg held both Addy and Morgan close before they could dash off into the Library. Born here in the Fae Realm, the two young girls knew nothing else besides having the Great Library as both a nanny and place to freely play.

Munch and Brigid stood side-by-side, likely already plotting to dash off on a mission of their own as soon as Viola and Sebastian left.

Beatrice blinked rapidly and hugged a red bookwyrm to her. If only Viola didn't have to leave her little sister behind.

Viola couldn't be there for all her siblings. Right now, Sebastian needed her. Beatrice would be all right, here in the Great Library, looked after by Basil, Meg, Munch, and Brigid.

All the goodbyes had already been said. There was nothing else to do but to give one last smile, turn, and face the wall filled with Anywhere Doors, one of which would take her away from her family.

This wasn't going to be for forever. She would see her family again. They would only be a step through an Anywhere Door away.

That didn't make the first step away from them any easier to take.

Sebastian led the way to the nearest Anywhere Door, an excited briskness to his steps. As he put a hand on the door, he leaned closer. "I cannot wait for you to finally see the Island of Melyria. There's someone there I want you to meet."

Viola halted and blinked up at him. He was grinning from ear to ear, a gleam in blue eyes the same shade as hers. "Wait, did you meet someone? Why haven't you mentioned her before?"

Sebastian shrugged, his grin still wide. "It's complicated. But you'll meet her soon."

Viola sighed and shook her head. "You used to tell me everything. The Fae Realm has made you sneaky."

"I have reasons." Sebastian gripped the latch, then opened the Anywhere Door for them. The door frame outlined a white stone pavilion surrounded by lush trees and overlooking crashing ocean waves. "Ladies first."

Viola glanced over her shoulder one last time, as she took her first step toward the Anywhere Door.

Even as Viola crossed the threshold, Queen Hippolyta spun, drawing her sword. King Theseus reacted a heartbeat later, drawing his own sword. Basil shoved Meg and their daughters behind him. Munch whipped out his bow. There seemed to be shouts, growing faint and distant as the Anywhere Door yanked at Viola.

Time. Space. Distance. It all seemed to stretch, tugging her in all directions. Normally stepping through an Anywhere Door was a nearly instantaneous thing, a mere shiver marking the passing through the linking magic.

This time, the magic frayed around her. She struggled to move, a part of her knowing that if she didn't move, she would be torn apart as the two courts yanked away from each other.

Then Sebastian shoved her, and she tumbled out the far side into the white pavilion, still clutching the basket to her chest. Inside, the bookwyrms were chirruping and scrambling about in a sign of their fear and panic.

She caught one glimpse of Sebastian, his face white, his hand reaching for her, before the Anywhere Door snapped shut behind her.

"Sebastian!" She scrambled to her feet and lunged for the door. She gripped the latch and yanked. Hard.

The Anywhere Door wouldn't open. No matter how hard she tugged, it was locked tight.

Chapter Two

Favian Orsino, Duke of the Island of Melyria, strolled along the cobbled road above the grassy bank that dipped down into the grassy beach below. If not for having to meet the new librarians shortly, he would have taken off his shoes to shuffle through the sand.

Instead, he kept his boots on, his white shirt pristine, though he had left his coat behind in his study. As he entered the outskirts of the seaside village, he let the bustle and noise close around him. At the docks, the fishing boats tied off at their allotted piers, ready to unload their morning's catches of fish. Peasant wives and the servants of nobility descended on the boats, bartering for the best prices for the prized catches.

As the cobbled street wound up the side of the steep bluffs, all of the houses were built of the same stone covered with white stucco plaster and roofed with red tiles, a contrast with the turquoise waters of the ocean twinkling in the sunlight.

He nodded at a few of his people as he passed, but he couldn't seem to find anything to say.

His father would have known exactly what to say. He would have known everyone's name, the names of their children, their entire life's story.

Instead, all Favian could do was nod and take in the sight of his people going about their day. A sprite wearing a pink dress that nearly matched her pink skin swept her front step. A goblin woman with a pig's snout and ears flapped out her laundry, spilling droplets of water into the crisp morning air, before she hung it over a line to dry. A group of fauns trotted by, their hooves clattering on the cobbles, as they hustled to their jobs along the wharf.

Above the village, his palace perched on the highest hill on this part of the island, a grand mansion of white stucco and a red, clay tiled roof. Columned porches surrounded the entire palace while all the tall windows were open to let in the sea breezes, wafting in the scents of fish, salt, and warm sand.

Favian drew in a deep breath, then released it slowly, trying to ease the ever-present tension in his shoulders.

In the two years since he'd had the mantle of duke placed upon him by his father's death, he couldn't seem to relax. His father had left large boots to fill, and the duty to make sure Melyria remained an idyllic island home for its inhabitants—a safe place in the normally turbulent Fae Realm—rested on Favian's shoulders.

The tension in his shoulders eased back to manageable as he stepped onto the porch of his palace. He didn't even have to knock before his butler opened the door for him, bowing as Favian stepped inside.

Favian strode through the halls until he stepped into his

spacious study. One wall held large, tall windows that over-looked the village, the beach, and the ocean beyond. The other sides were filled with built-in shelves.

Shelves that stood empty, now that the accumulated book collection of the dukes of Melyria had been donated to the new outpost library.

There was just something achingly sad about those empty shelves, even though he knew all the books were going to a good home that wasn't far away. The books would do far more good for his people in an outpost library than sitting here in his study.

Still, he would need to find other items to fill the shelves. He had never been one for knickknacks, but an exception would have to be made in this case.

He sank into the chair behind his desk. He had a few minutes before he had to meet the librarians, and he might as well tackle one of the neat stacks of paperwork on his desk.

A knock made him jump. His arm caught one of the stacks of paperwork, spreading it in disarray across his desk. He took a moment to straighten the papers before he looked up.

His sprite servant Cesario—his navy suit nearly matching the indigo of his hair—stood in the doorway. At only three feet tall, the blue-skinned sprite's head was level with the door's latch.

"Your Grace, I apologize for the interruption." Cesario gave a little cough.

"It's all right." Favian pushed to his feet. "I know. I need to leave to meet the librarians."

"Yes, but that isn't why I am here. Or, at least, not the only reason I am here." Cesario pulled a crisp, white envelope from his starched pocket. "You have a message from Lady Olivia."

Favian forced himself to coolly take the note instead of lunging and snatching it from Cesario's fingers.

Turning to his seat, he opened the note, heart rising into his throat. It promptly sank into his stomach as he read the words on the page.

She still refused to see him. Which was terribly inconvenient, because they were supposed to be getting married. Their fathers had made a bargain just over two years ago that Favian and Olivia would wed.

A bargain had been made, so a bargain had to be kept. Favian would marry Olivia, and that would be that.

He had no compunctions against the marriage. In fact, it fit quite nicely into his well-ordered life. A neatly arranged marriage. A neatly arranged island. Even a new outpost library, to encourage the citizens to further their minds and embrace order instead of the tendency toward relaxed chaos that often characterized the Court of Islands.

Only two things had ever upset Favian's carefully laid organization for his life.

His father's untimely death, and Olivia's stubborn refusal to see Favian.

Granted, her father, too, had been killed in the same shipwreck that killed his father. She had reason to mourn.

But it had been two whole years. And Favian had been rather patient, after all.

A bargain was a bargain. Such things were dangerous to leave undone like this.

Olivia knew that. It was one thing for her to risk herself, but he was the duke of their island now. He wasn't just risking himself but the whole island by not finishing the bargain.

More than that, chaos on their island could spread to the entire Court of Islands, if they weren't careful. Perhaps the islands weren't as united as many courts since they didn't have a single monarch but a conglomerate of dukes and duchesses, but they were still a single court. Trouble on one island affected all the islands.

The Fae Realm had been especially disorderly lately. It would not take much for the chaos to spread to the Court of Islands. If that happened, Favian would be rather put out.

Favian suppressed a sigh and pushed away from his desk. Surely Olivia would come out of her grief soon.

Especially now that the outpost library would be established twelve nights from now. The outpost library had, after all, been her idea. Starting two years ago shortly after their fathers had died, she had asked Favian for such a thing here on the island. Still mourning his father, Favian had not been able to focus on bringing that about for several months.

But now he had finally completed the negotiations with King Theseus, and the librarians would arrive shortly. If anything could prove to Olivia that Favian was serious and pull her out of her sorrow, then seeing the library come to being would be it.

Standing, Favian grabbed his coat from the back of his chair, shrugged into it, and strolled through the palace, nodding at a few of the servants as they glided about, efficiently conducting their duties.

The lower section of the palace opened to a broad porch that wrapped around three sides of the palace, held up with large columns. Various gardens flowed into the mountain around the palace, sectioning off different pavilions and outbuildings.

Favian strode down the steps into one of the gardens, this one surrounding a pavilion formed of white columns. Inside the pavilion, an Anywhere Door stood inside a stone arch.

A slim girl in a gray skirt, white shirt, and green coat yanked on the Anywhere Door. A basket sat near her feet with several blue bookwyrms peeking over the rim. Her light blonde hair and pale skin were rare colors to see on the islands where skin tones ranged from his sun-kissed tan to dark brown. Or shades of blue, pink, green, and other colors for the sprites and other fae races.

Favian strolled down the steps to the pavilion and cleared his throat. "Welcome to the Court of Islands. I am Duke Favian Orsino."

The girl made a noise in the back of her throat and whirled to face him. She was gasping for breath, her deep blue eyes set in a white face. "I…yes. I'm Librarian Viola."

She seemed a rather jumpy thing. But perhaps that came from being a sheltered librarian. A human one, at that. He had been warned that the two librarians assigned to this outpost would be humans. He didn't have a problem with humans, per se. Except for a certain human pirate he'd banned from Melyria two years ago on pain of death.

"I was expecting two librarians. Has Librarian Sebastian arrived?" Favian swept a glance around, but he didn't see the librarian. Which was odd, since Librarian Sebastian had done all the negotiating on King Theseus's behalf.

If anything, Librarian Viola's face turned whiter still as she stared back at him, her ocean-blue eyes stark against her pallor.

Something rose inside his chest at the sight. A twinge. An urge to step forward.

Perhaps it was indigestion. His breakfast must not be sitting well.

VIOLA BLINKED at the fae lord before her. He stared at her with a forbidding glower lowering his brows over his dark eyes. His black hair lay pristinely combed over his tanned forehead, adding to his dour mien. Why hadn't Sebastian warned her that the duke of the island was so disagreeable?

Sebastian… Her heart twisted. Had Sebastian tumbled back into the Hall of Anywhere Doors? Or was he lost between the realms?

Worse, what if he was dead? What if…

She could not think about that. She had to believe that Sebastian was alive, either lost or back in the Court of Knowledge with the rest of her family.

Either way, the Anywhere Door wasn't working, leaving her stuck on this island, and there was nothing she could do about it. As a human, she didn't have the knowledge or magic to fix the Anywhere Door. With the Door broken, she couldn't look for Sebastian. She was alone here, cut off from her family and helpless to do a thing about it.

By the way the fae lord was glaring at her, she wasn't sure she dared trust him to ask for his help. Outside of the Court of Knowledge, she'd come across very few trustworthy people among the fae, especially among the fae nobility. Most fae nobles were either flighty, like King Oberon and Queen Titania of the Court of Revels, or downright evil, like Lord Chauvlyn, her sister Brigid's nemesis. Until she knew Duke Orsino better, she couldn't trust him.

The fae lord glanced around again, that frown deepening further. "I expected Librarian Sebastian would be here to oversee the founding of the library."

What would he do if she told him that Sebastian hadn't made it through the Anywhere Door? What if he called the whole thing off and discontinued his support for an outpost library? After all, Sebastian was supposed to be the head librarian here, and fae nobles were particularly fickle.

This outpost library had been Sebastian's dream. She couldn't let it fall apart just because he wasn't here.

Unless—she gripped the amber pendant of the glamour necklace—what if Sebastian could be here? While Duke Orsino had worked with Sebastian over the past two years to set up this outpost, he probably didn't know him *well*. All he had was a brief, business acquaintance. Maybe it was a bad first impression, but Duke Orsino didn't seem the type to get to know those who he believed were beneath him.

She could do this. She couldn't do anything for Sebastian wherever he was, but she could pretend to be Sebastian and preserve his dream. Doing something—even something small like founding the outpost library—was better than sitting around helplessly worrying.

"I..." She waved vaguely as she tried to gather her thoughts and her composure. With a deep breath, she drew herself straighter. "I'll go get him. Wait here a moment."

She raced around the back of the Anywhere Door. It was the nearest cover she could find, and it would give her—well, Sebastian—a handy excuse for being out of sight.

Viola glanced around. The space behind the Anywhere Door was shadowed by the door and arch while hedges for the gardens grew tall enough to hide her back here. There was only a small strip of paving stones back here. Just enough room for her.

Gripping the pendant, she squeezed her eyes shut and envisioned her brother. Sebastian. Tall. Blond-haired. Always grinning. Always looking out for her and Beatrice.

A shivery, filmy sensation washed over her. It was almost claustrophobic, and she had to concentrate to breathe past it. Something almost like a second skin plastered to her, tight and clinging and invisible.

Or—as she opened her eyes—not so invisible. When she glanced down at herself, she didn't see her small hands, her figure. She was taller. Her brother's large hands gripped the pendant over his light gray shirt, which was tucked into darker gray trousers.

Then her vision went cross-eyed as she saw double. Both her brother's clothes, and her own. Her own hands, and yet his. It was dizzying.

With a deep breath, she tucked the pendant beneath her shirt and straightened her shoulders, trying not to shiver at the cloying feeling of the magic sticking to her.

She was Sebastian. Think manly thoughts.

With her shoulders back, she forced herself to lengthen her strides and strut in a manly, assured way around the Anywhere Door.

Duke Orsino turned to her as she appeared. "Librarian Sebastian. It is good to see that you have arrived."

Viola resisted the urge to release a breath of relief. Apparently Duke Orsino didn't know Sebastian well enough to instantly see through the glamour.

She started to reach for her dress for a curtsy, then stopped herself and managed to change the move into a bow instead. She was Sebastian. Be Sebastian. Move like him. Talk like him.

Right now, she was the head librarian of this outpost reporting to the lord of this island. She would have to tell him some of what was going on, even if she didn't trust him enough to tell him everything or ask for his help. "Yes, though it was a near thing. There seems to be a problem with the Anywhere Door. After I—we—stepped through, it slammed shut, and it won't open."

Duke Orsino's brows lowered even further. But he didn't step forward and try the Door himself, as she had expected he would.

Oh, right. He had another man tell him that the Door wasn't working. So he took Sebastian at his word, instead of trying the door himself as he would have if Viola had told him.

That was new. Not being doubted, even subconsciously.

Instead, Duke Orsino focused on her. "What do you believe is the problem?"

Uh, what did she think was the problem? At this point, she had no clue. She hadn't even had a chance to absorb what had just happened.

But she was pretending to be Sebastian, who had supposedly spent the last few minutes inspecting the Door. As a librarian of the Court of Knowledge—the Court responsible for the Doors—Sebastian would be expected to have some understanding of the Doors, even if he wouldn't have the magic to be able to sense what was going on the way a fae might.

"I don't think there is an issue with the Anywhere Door here." She gestured toward the Door, her thoughts solidifying even as she spoke. "There was some kind of commotion in the Hall of Anywhere Doors as we were leaving. I suspect that the issue is back there."

Even as she spoke, the words sat heavy in her gut. If the issue was back in the Court of Knowledge, then her whole family was in danger, not just Sebastian.

And, worst of all, there was absolutely nothing she could do to help any of them. Sure, she could rush off, find a berth on an outgoing ship, hope she didn't end up carried off by fae pirates, and stumble blindly into whatever trouble was going on back home. If she tried that, she would just get herself into more trouble and danger.

Right now, she was safe. It would be far smarter to stay where she was, do what she had come to do, and attempt to learn what she could before she did anything more.

"Then there is nothing we can do until King Theseus corrects the problem." Duke Orsino glowered at the Door for a long moment before he turned back to her. "Thankfully you and your sister arrived safely before the issue shut down the Door. I will show you and your sister to your accommodations."

Viola froze. How was she going to explain her absence? Or Sebastian's absence? She couldn't be both of them at the same time.

Ugh, this was already getting complicated, and it had only been a few minutes.

But something was wrong with the Anywhere Door. Sebastian was missing. And Viola didn't dare tell anyone that Sebastian was missing until she figured out what was going on.

She jabbed a finger at the Anywhere Door. "I would like to stay and inspect the Door further. But Viola will go with you. I'll go get her."

It was so strange to talk about herself in the third person.

Without waiting for Duke Orsino to reply, she started to dash behind the Anywhere Door, remembered that she needed to dash like a man, and slowed her pace to a relaxed stroll.

How obvious could she be, darting back and forth around the Door? Hopefully the duke was a particularly oblivious person. Or he would chalk up their oddities to their humanity. After all, it wasn't like he would expect humans to possess a glamour.

Once she was safely behind the Door, she took the pendant out from underneath her shirt.

As soon as the pendant lost contact with her skin, that slimy, filmy feeling vanished, and she could finally take a decent breath again. Her hands were once again her own. Her clothes were her own. She was herself, and she hadn't realized how much of a relief that would be.

This whole pretending to be her brother thing was going to be harder than she thought.

Chapter Three

Viola popped out from behind the Anywhere Door and smoothed her skirt. She picked up the basket with the sapling and bookwyrms, hugged it to her, and faced Duke Orsino. "Sebastian said you were going to show me to the outpost library?"

Duke Orsino gave a sharp nod, spun on his heel in a precise manner, and strode toward the palace that perched on the hill above the pavilion.

Viola hurried after him, pausing partway up the hill to glance back at the Anywhere Door one last time. Was Sebastian all right? Was he stuck between the realms? Was the rest of her family all right?

She shook her head and forced herself to keep moving. Right now, she was cut off from everything and everyone. All she could do was make the best of it and try to salvage what she could of Sebastian's dream. She would have to trust that Sebastian could take care of himself, wherever he was. He was certainly more capable of rescuing himself than she was of doing anything to help him.

Duke Orsino led the way up the short flight of stairs to the columned porch that ran along three sides of the palace. Instead of going inside the palace, he strolled along the porch, passing benches that had been placed in the best spots to enjoy the view and the breezes while staying in the shade. Flower boxes stood between columns, overflowing with blooms and trailing greenery.

Viola resisted the urge to gape. From where the palace stood on the hill, the rest of the island flowed into rolling green hills bordered by turquoise waters. A strip of sandy beach bordered a curving bay while cliffs rose from the sea around the rest of the island she could see. The town below the palace had been built in layers of white buildings with red, clay tile roofs. Other stone buildings dotted the island.

A few fae bustled about on the island. Some were mostly human-looking, but others had skin in shades of pastels or flowers growing in their hair. A few birds shedding sparkling trails of glitter flitted overhead.

She had never seen anything like this. In her childhood, she had grown up on a dusty, failing farm. Then she had spent her adolescent years in the forested Court of Knowledge.

What adventure would Viola experience here in the Court of Islands?

Hopefully, not much of one. All she wanted to do was start the outpost library, look after the bookwyrms, and live a quiet, not-adventurous life. With her brother Sebastian at her side, looking out for her as he always did.

This was already more adventure than she'd bargained for. She was here alone. Sebastian was missing. The responsibility for the outpost library fell solely on her shoulders.

Swallowing, she hurried to catch up with Duke Orsino.

He had such long legs, and he strode with a long, purposeful stride as if unworried that those with shorter legs might struggle to keep up.

At the end of the long porch, another set of stairs led down into yet another garden. Butterflies with iridescent wings of vibrant colors flitted between the flowers, leaving trails of sparkles shining briefly in the sunlight behind them. A few dragonflies—mini dragon-shaped bodies with buzzing wings—hovered over the tiny pond in the center, puffing tiny tongues of flame.

Belch, one of the more adventurous bookwyrms, peeked his head farther over the edge of the basket, and he snapped at one of the dragonflies as it buzzed past. The dragonfly's buzz increased, and it puffed a breath of fire in retaliation. Belch returned with his own, larger puff of fire.

Viola hurried down the path, turning the basket before the dragonfly or the bookwyrm set anything on fire in their feud.

At the far end of the garden, a round building made of the same white stone lay at the end of one of the looping, white gravel paths. Instead of red tile, this building had a glass roof.

"This is the outpost library." Duke Orsino gestured to the round building with a controlled motion. "It was built to King Theseus's specifications, as provided by your brother Sebastian."

Then it was sure to be precisely correct. Duke Orsino didn't seem to be the type to deviate from directions even an iota.

"It looks lovely." Viola glanced at him. When he made no move toward the outpost library, she eased past him, then led the way along the marble path through the garden. When she reached the building, she climbed up the steps.

The oak door remained elegant despite being a plain, dark wood, free of carvings, with a simple, wrought iron handle. Somehow, the plainness made it seem even more tasteful.

Propping the basket on her hip, she lifted the handle, then pushed the door open.

Inside, the building was a single, cavernous space, though she couldn't see far since shelves curved in concentric rings that formed a maze of passages. Sunlight beamed through the glass dome ceiling, splashing patterns on the floor and empty shelves.

More empty wooden shelves lined the outer wall while stained-glass windows were set between the shelves, adding light and patterns to the kaleidoscope on the floor. Window seats were built into the space beneath each of the windows, forming cozy nooks where readers could curl up with a book.

Most of the floor was formed of white marble paving stones with dirt in between. Occasionally, a round mosaic set into the stone showed a scene of a tree or a flower.

Viola glanced at Duke Orsino, then set out among the shelves, following the curving paths round and round until they spiraled into the open space in the center of this outpost library.

Here a patch in the direct center beneath the dome had been left as bare dirt, waiting for the cutting from the Great Library's tree to be planted.

Duke Orsino's clipped pace rang against the tiling stones behind her before he halted at the end of one of the shelves.

"Does the outpost meet with your specifications, Lady Librarian?"

She was hardly a lady, but Viola wasn't going to argue with him. Giving her a title that wasn't really hers was far better than disdain toward humans.

Instead, Viola smiled and set down the basket. "It looks suitable to me, but I'm not the ones we need to ask. What do you think, wyrmies?"

The bookwyrms poked their heads out, their ruffs flapping as their tongues darted in and out. Curio slithered over the edge of the basket, landing on the dirt of the outpost library. The bookwyrm's ruff fully extended as it looked around, its bright teal eyes unblinking. Belch was the next to plop out of the basket, followed by Toby, the darkest blue in color, and Feste, the smallest and only female. All four of them disappeared among the empty shelves.

As if sensing the delicacy of the moment, Duke Orsino remained standing where he was, silent and still as a statue.

Viola held still as well, letting the bookwyrms explore the space. After several long minutes, the bookwyrms slithered back into the light under the skylight. Their ruffs had gone back down, and Curio slid up to her and bumped her ankle, giving the rasping grumbling sound that was almost a purr. Feste and Toby twined around the basket while Belch faced Duke Orsino and burped, the puff of smoke accompanied by the stench of roasted rodent. Apparently the bookwyrm had already found a pest to nosh on while exploring.

No matter the fancy magic or protective enchantments, even the Fae Realm had a mouse problem.

Viola smiled, knelt, and scratched Curio behind his ruff. "Looks like the bookwyrms approve."

Duke Orsino gave a solemn tip of his chin. "Very well. Is there anything you will need for them?"

"No, they are pretty self-sufficient." Even as Viola stood, Toby's ruff stood up again, then he slithered off in a hurry, disappearing once again among the shelves.

"I see." Duke Orsino pushed away from the shelves, then gestured toward an opening in the shelves across the way. "The crates with books are back there."

After picking up the basket with the tiny sapling once again, Viola strolled in that direction, spiraling through the shelves until she reached the far wall.

There, two doorways bracketed a darkened section of wall piled high with crates.

Duke Orsino gestured to the crates. "I did not order them organized on the shelves since I assumed you and your brother would wish to take on the task."

"Yes, we would." Viola mentally tried to calculate how many books would be inside those crates. Probably not enough to fully fill all the shelves, but extra space on bookshelves for more books was always a good thing. It would still be a lot of work by herself, especially since she couldn't admit that it was just her tackling the work. "You must have been collecting for a while."

Duke Orsino gave a slight shrug. "Most of this is from my personal collection. It was doing little good hidden away in the palace's study. I will, of course, continue to add to the outpost's collection as I have opportunity to do so."

"I—we—will organize the books with room for expansion in mind." Viola lapsed into silence, not sure what else to say to the staid fae lord.

After the moment of silence dragged on just long enough to turn awkward, Duke Orsino rocked back onto his heels before he gestured at the two doors. "These are your rooms."

"I am sure we will find them satisfactory." Viola shifted her grip on the basket. She did not dare explore the rooms until Duke Orsino left.

As if sensing that this was his moment to give her space, Duke Orsino gave a sharp kind of nod. "I will leave you to get settled. If you or your brother need anything, do not hesitate to ask."

Viola forced a smile and nodded in return. What she needed was to know what was going on back home in the Court of Knowledge and what had happened to her brother.

Those were questions Duke Orsino couldn't answer. Nor did Viola even dare let the duke know what was going on.

Duke Orsino spun on his heel and started to march away. At the first of the shelves, he wheeled back to her for a moment. "When your brother returns from inspecting the Anywhere Door, please have him report to me, if he doesn't go directly to the palace."

Viola gritted her teeth and resisted the urge to touch the glamour necklace. "Of course. I'm sure he was already planning to report to you."

Well, he was now. She would have to inspect the rooms here, then gather the courage to glamour herself into Sebastian again to make a report.

What would she tell Duke Orsino? She didn't know what was going on. What would Sebastian—the real Sebastian—have figured out and reported to Duke Orsino?

Neither she nor Sebastian was fae. They couldn't sense the magic of the Anywhere Doors, much less truly inspect it. But Sebastian—the real Sebastian—probably had a better idea of how the Anywhere Doors worked than she did. He had always been interested in that side of things more than she had been.

The fae lord gave her one last nod, then disappeared among the shelves once again.

She waited for several long heartbeats before she released a long, slow breath. She didn't dare stop moving, otherwise she would just break down into tears.

Gripping the basket with the tree in one arm, she pushed open the door on the right and stepped inside.

The small, round room boasted white columns rising to a domed ceiling. Between the columns, tall windows gave views of the cliffs and the turquoise sea beyond. The walls that weren't filled with windows had been painted in murals of oceanside villages that moved, the people in the scenes going about their own business, utterly noiseless. None of them looked outward, which helped the moving scene remain charming rather than giving her the skittering feeling that someone was watching her.

A canopied bed, draped in blue silks, stood along one of the walls with a table beside the bed and an armoire along another wall. Other than that, the room was empty of furniture.

When she checked the second room, it was identical to the first, except for slight differences in the murals.

Was there any kind of cleaning staff? Or did this outpost clean itself, the way the House back home did?

If she noticed anyone coming in and out, she would have to make both rooms look as lived in as possible to keep up the pretense that both she and Sebastian were here.

She sank onto the bed, clutching the basket to her. What had happened to Sebastian? Was he back in the Court of

Knowledge? Or was he stuck somewhere between the realms?

All she could do was wonder. She couldn't rescue him. She couldn't even find out what had happened to him. All she could do was pretend to be both herself and Sebastian until all this was sorted out, one way or another.

And maybe give in to a tear or two and have a good cry. Viola curled over the basket, a sob working her way up her throat. After all, it wasn't like Duke Orsino would be able to see that she had been crying when she reported to him in the Sebastian glamour.

Perhaps tears wouldn't solve anything. But right now, she was alone and helpless to do anything. At least crying was something she *could* do.

SEBASTIAN CURLED ON THE GROUND—IF it could be called ground in this tangled place. It was like being stuck inside of the wavering shimmer cast by the sun over water on the hottest of summer days. Everything around him shook and tumbled, tearing at him until he couldn't tell which way was up or down.

How long had he lain here? Moments? Days? Eons? There was no such thing as time or space or distance here in this place-that-wasn't-really-a-place between the realms.

He could lie here. For a few minutes. For forever. There was no difference.

If he stayed here, he would never move again. He would die, lost in the between and torn apart by the worlds.

He couldn't die. Viola was somewhere out there. Was she stuck between the realms with him? He cracked his eyes open, trying to peer through the haze. He couldn't see her. He scraped his hand over the ground, patting the space around him. No one lay nearby.

Did that mean she had made it to the Court of Islands? If so, then she was safe enough, at least for now. But she was all alone in the Court of Islands, trying to start the outpost library all by herself.

She didn't know Duke Orsino or anyone else on the island. She didn't know all the connections he had made.

Then there was his family back in the Court of Knowledge. Something had been happening as they were stepping into the Anywhere Door. Had the court been under attack? Was his family in danger? Munch and Brigid would be fine, whatever came. Basil and Meg could be rather formidable, when backed into a corner. But they had their daughters to think of. Then there was Beatrice, only seventeen.

Sebastian drew deep within himself and inched a hand forward. Then the other. It felt like the weight of the worlds rested on his back as he shifted his knee and scraped forward over the ground beneath him. If it was ground. Maybe he was crawling along the sky.

He didn't know which way he had to go. Perhaps direction mattered less than intent in this case.

All he knew was that he couldn't stop. He had to keep crawling, even if that meant inching along like a worm on his belly. That was the only way he had a hope—wispy as it was—to get out of here.

Chapter Four

Viola brushed off her skirt and surveyed her handiwork. Once she had finished her good cry, she had unpacked several of the crates—under the supervision of Feste who had remained with the sapling —and sorted through a few of the books.

But she had delayed long enough. She had to report to Duke Orsino on the inspection of the Anywhere Door.

Gripping the glamour necklace, she closed her eyes and envisioned Sebastian. That clingy feeling wrapped around her again, and she tucked the amber beneath her bodice. Shirt. Whatever it was.

She glanced at where two bookwyrms, Curio and Feste, curled next to the basket with the sapling. She wasn't supposed to leave it out of her sight. But so far, Duke Orsino had only seen her as Viola with the tree. Would it look strange if she, as Sebastian, brought it to their meeting? If Sebastian were really here, he would have left the tree with her.

How much of a risk would it be to leave the tree here

under the guard of the bookwyrms? There had been trouble back in the Court of Knowledge as they were leaving, but everything seemed peaceful here on this island, even if she didn't trust its duke. And they were currently cut off from any trouble that might be brewing.

It would be a risk no matter what she did. Perhaps it would be best to find a hiding spot for the tree here in the outpost. She couldn't haul it around with her everywhere for the next twelve days. It had been feasible when there were supposed to be two of them, so one person could go out while the other stayed with the outpost and the tree. But that was no longer possible. She might put the tree more at risk if she carried it all over the place with her.

If only she could have just stuffed the sapling into her magical pocket. But living things like plants, animals, or people couldn't go in magical pockets—not if one wanted those things to stay living, anyway.

Where could she hide the tree in the library? It was so empty and blank. In the Great Library with its living tree, she could have asked the Library to swallow something into the walls, and it would be well hidden.

Here, the tree wasn't yet grown and couldn't be planted until the full moon on the twelfth night. Until then, the outpost building was just that…a dead building.

Glancing around, she finally tucked the tree at the back of one of the bottom shelves, then placed a row of books in front of it. It wasn't the best hiding spot right now, since these were rather obviously the only books on the shelves. But once she unpacked and organized more of the books, the hiding spot would get better. Perhaps she could use some of the wood from the crates to create a false back of a shelf or something. Not that she was particularly skilled when it came to such stuff. Building necessities out of scraps was always Sebastian's thing more than hers.

For now, this would have to be good enough.

Viola spun on her heel and started for the door, only to pause and straighten her shoulders. She had to remember to walk like Sebastian, not like herself.

March. She was a guy. Long strides. Head high. Swagger, not sway.

She strode from the outpost library, along the path, and into the palace. If she really was Sebastian, then she would know where Duke Orsino's study was. She would have met with him there several times.

Strolling along the hallway, she peered around while trying to pretend she knew exactly where she was going.

The seaside palace was beautiful. Most of the large windows were propped open, letting in the sea breezes that stirred the sheer white curtains. Blue runners lined the hallways while the walls featured mural after mural of pastoral scenes that moved in the peaceful bustle of island life just like the ones in her room.

As she turned a corner, she nearly ran into a blue-skinned sprite with long, tapered ears tufted with darker blue fur that matched the indigo hair that was neatly combed into a precise, center part. He wore a three-piece suit in shades of blue.

The sprite smiled and gave her a little bow. "Librarian Sebastian, it is good to have you back."

Right. She was Sebastian. And apparently Sebastian knew this sprite. She smiled, wiping the blank nonrecognition from her face, and gave what she hoped looked like a manly nod in return. "It is good to be back. Is Duke Orsino in his study?"

It was a risk since she had no idea if she was wandering in the right section of the palace. Hopefully the question would nudge the sprite to lead her to the study.

The sprite nodded, not giving any indication that he thought the question odd. "Yes, as he usually is."

As she had hoped, the sprite turned and set off down the hallway with the clear expectation that she—well, Sebastian —would follow.

Now if she could only figure out the sprite's name before she gave away that she didn't actually know him.

Favian stared down at the note on his desk. Yet another message from Olivia, refusing to see him.

This was getting ridiculous. Their fathers' bargain left them no wiggle room. They had to get married. There was nothing to be done about that. It would be foolish to continue ignoring each other.

He didn't think Olivia hated him. They had always gotten along well, up until two years ago. What had changed? Was it truly that she needed space after her father's death? Or was something else going on? He wouldn't know until he talked with her.

He had done all this for her. The outpost library. Inviting the human librarians here.

A knock sounded on the door, and his clerk Cesario popped his head in. "Librarian Sebastian is here to speak with you."

"Show him in." Favian stuffed the note under other paperwork, then leaned back in his seat behind his desk.

Sebastian strolled inside, wearing his standard dark gray

trousers, lighter gray shirt, and the black librarian coat that marked him as a master librarian. He hesitated before the desk, bending in a hint of a bow, then pausing, as if he was not sure if he should bow or sit or simply stand there.

Favian gestured, indicating for Sebastian to take the seat across from him. "What did you learn from your examination of the Anywhere Door?"

Librarian Sebastian slid onto the chair and crossed his legs. Then he froze, shifted, and quickly uncrossed his legs, slouched a bit, and spread out his knees, all the while fidgeting.

Odd. Favian shook his head and blinked. The librarian must not have good news to share. He seemed far more jumpy than he had been the last time Favian had spoken with him.

After another moment of shifting, the librarian seemed to gather himself and rested his hands on his knees. "The Anywhere Door still won't open, and there doesn't appear to be anything wrong with the Door on this end."

"Hmm." Favian leaned farther back in his chair and pondered that. "The Court of Knowledge has protections on the Anywhere Doors. They implemented them against the Court of Revels two years ago. I don't think King Theseus would do so against the Court of Islands while two of his librarians were stepping through a Door. Unless circumstances were dire indeed back in the Court of Knowledge."

"That's what I'm afraid of." Sebastian hugged his arms to his stomach before he shifted and returned to bracing them against his knees. "We're cut off from the Court of Knowledge, at least for now."

"I'll send a message by boat to the Island of Nettis to see

if their Anywhere Door is working." Favian tapped his fingers on his desk.

"My sister Viola could write a message to Queen Hippolyta of the Court of Swordmaidens. If you could find a way to get a message to her island, she would know what is going on, if anyone does." Sebastian flexed his fingers on his knees.

"That is a good idea. I can arrange for a female messenger." Favian would have to see if Cesario had any suggestions on who to send. The Court of Swordmaidens only allowed women to step foot on their island, except on very rare and limited occasions. "There is nothing more we can do while we wait for information. Will the situation with the Court of Knowledge and the Anywhere Door cause any difficulties for you and your sister as you set up the outpost library?"

Sebastian swallowed but shook his head. "I—we—are worried about our family in the Court of Knowledge. And I wish we didn't have to set up the outpost without any access to the Great Library. But the situation won't affect our work."

"Good." Favian nodded. He was not unduly worried. King Theseus and the Court of Knowledge had proven to be quite resilient in the past few years, especially since King Theseus married Queen Hippolyta of the Court of Swordmaidens. Whatever the trouble, they likely could handle it.

Until then, he had his own troubles to worry about. Namely, what to do about Olivia and his father's bargain.

Unfulfilled bargains were dangerous. The Laws of Bargains and Bindings wouldn't let him skirt around it. His court could find itself destroyed, ripped apart at the seams, if he worked against such a bargain.

With an unknown situation in the Court of Knowledge, instability in the Court of Revels, and rumblings of danger coming from the Realm of Monsters, this was no time to let a bargain lie undone.

Olivia knew that, and yet she was avoiding him. He couldn't even ask her what was going on and what he could do to fix it if she wouldn't talk to him.

This was so unlike Olivia. She loved the island, as he did. He had always liked that about her. They'd grown up together, the son of the ruling duke and the daughter of his most prominent advisor. They had promenaded through these halls, so young yet already pretending they were grown. That girl he had grown up with would never put the whole island at risk like this.

Favian regarded Sebastian. The librarian was smart. Most librarians were. The outpost library had been Olivia's dream. Perhaps she wouldn't talk to Favian or any of his servants, but surely she would talk to one of the outpost librarians.

Sending Sebastian's sister Viola would have been preferable, but Sebastian would do.

"While we wait for news, there is a little matter you can help me with." Favian leaned his elbows on his desk.

Across the way, Sebastian eyed him, a frown puckering his expression. "Yes?"

Favian cleared his throat, resisting the urge to tug at his collar. How did one go about asking something like this? But something had to be done before the chaos of a broken bargain jeopardized his island. "Lady Olivia was instrumental in organizing the outpost library. Tomorrow, could you carry a message to her from me? You can assure her that the outpost library is in good hands."

"Of course, my lord." Sebastian gave an attempt at a bow while he was sitting down.

"I will send Cesario over with the note in the morning." Once Favian had written it. And re-written it. Perhaps he should have Sebastian write the note as well. He likely had a much better gift for words than Favian did. "Cesario can retrieve the note from your sister for Queen Hippolyta in the morning as well."

Sebastian gave a nod, though the pucker remained etched into his forehead, as if he remained confused by the request.

It was odd, to be sure. This was something Favian should be handling himself, not sending an outpost librarian to handle for him. Sebastian technically wasn't even a part of Favian's court. He didn't actually have the authority to order Sebastian to do this.

But Sebastian seemed agreeable enough. It wasn't a huge favor to ask.

After a long moment, Sebastian gripped the armrests, poised to stand. "If that is all, I should be going."

"Yes." Favian waved in dismissal. "I know you have a lot of work to accomplish in the outpost library."

Sebastian popped to his feet, took two scurrying steps to the door, before he paused, slowed, and returned to his usual saunter.

Something was odd with Sebastian. Perhaps it was just jitters now that the outpost library was a reality. Favian had heard that humans were more prone to nerves than most fae, but he had never had occasion to witness the human temperament up close like this before. Sebastian's sister Viola had also demonstrated the same nervous habits.

Hopefully Sebastian and Viola got over their nerves to conduct their duty properly. Favian had nothing against humans, but he had gone through a great deal of effort to establish this outpost library. King Theseus had assured him that these human librarians were among his best, and Favian had judged that those assurances weren't a clever trick by the librarian king. He was known to be one of the few good ones among the fae rulers.

It would be terribly disappointing to find out that his reputation had been a lie.

Chapter Five

Viola rolled out of bed to the sound of unfamiliar birds tweeting in the trees outside her window, the air smelling of warm sands and the sea rather than the magical forest of the Tanglewood. She had slept well, but the feather mattress wasn't the cushy moss she'd grown used to. Nor had this outpost library awakened her the way the House would have if she were home. Not that she missed getting dumped onto the floor first thing in the morning, but it was just another quirk that made the House her home.

How long would it be before the outpost felt like home? Would she ever feel at home here?

As long as Sebastian was missing and she was cut off from her family, she couldn't feel at home here. It was all she could do to stuff down the ever-present panic and go on with the pretense so that she could save Sebastian's job for him when he returned.

He would return. He had to. Anything else was unthinkable.

She checked on the tree she had stashed underneath her bed, finding it surrounded by all four bookwyrms. They lifted their heads, giving her little squiggles, blinks, and a burp from Belch.

She dressed, then hurried over to what should have been Sebastian's room and mussed the bed. She didn't have any of his clothes to toss around, but she did put out a few of her personal items—items like a painting of the family—to make the room appear lived in.

Once that was taken care of, she set to work unboxing more of the books and arranging them on the shelves. She had to get as much done this morning as possible, before Duke Orsino's servant showed up with the note to take to Lady Olivia.

Her own note to Queen Hippolyta was already written and waiting in her pocket. After returning from the meeting with the duke, she had composed the note in her head while unboxing more books. She had chosen her words carefully since she couldn't say anything directly about the fact that Sebastian was missing, just in case the messenger read the note. But Queen Hippolyta was clever. She would read between the lines. If she didn't, then Brigid would.

How long would it take for a ship to sail to the Island of Nettis, then on to the Island of Swordmaidens? Even assuming the Swordmaidens would allow the messenger access to the island and accept the note, how long would all that take? Would it be soon enough for Sebastian?

"Ahem."

Viola started and dropped the book she'd been holding. It bounced off her foot and landed face down on the floor, the pages bent and the cover splayed.

She hurriedly snatched it from the floor, smoothing the

pages and mentally apologizing to the book for dropping it. The damage didn't look too bad. If she set it beneath a stack of heavy books, the wrinkles should smooth out. Hopefully.

Setting the book on the shelf, she finally turned to the source of the voice that had startled her.

The three-foot-tall, blue-skinned Cesario stood there, his indigo hair neatly parted as precisely down the center as it had been yesterday. So different from Puck, the green-skinned sprite who worked for King Oberon of the Court of Revels.

Cesario gave a small cough. "Is your brother here? I have a note for him from Duke Orsino."

"Yes, I'll fetch him." Viola hurried around the corner and checked that Cesario hadn't followed her.

When she was sure she was alone, she gripped the necklace's pendant. Changing into Sebastian proved to be even easier this time, as if the repeated practice made the magic more familiar.

The sticky, clinging feeling still wasn't all that comfortable, even if she found it easier to ignore the sensation as she stuffed the pendant beneath her shirt and stepped around the bookshelves once again.

"Cesario." She—as Sebastian—gave the servant what she hoped was a manly nod-greeting.

Cesario didn't seem to see anything amiss, for he held out a sheet of paper. "Here is the message that my duke would like you to deliver to Lady Olivia."

Viola took the note, slipped it into her pocket, then pulled out the note she had written. While the glamour made her look like Sebastian, underneath she still wore her clothes with the magical pocket where she had stashed the note. "Here is the message for Queen Hippolyta."

Cesario bowed and took the note, putting it into his own, likely also magical, pocket.

Viola shifted, then forced herself to plant her feet in a more manly way. Would Sebastian know the way to Lady Olivia's house, wherever she lived? If Viola asked Cesario for directions, she might give away that something was off, and Cesario might start seeing beneath the glamour.

On the other hand, if Sebastian didn't know the way, would Cesario think it odd that she—well, he—hadn't asked for directions yet?

No, Sebastian wouldn't ask for directions. He would be confident that he could find his way.

If Cesario knew that Sebastian didn't know where Lady Olivia lived, then surely he would offer the information of how to get there. Seeing that the note was delivered was part of Cesario's job, and he seemed to be thorough enough to think through something like directions.

She would just have to muddle through this on her own, pretending that she knew exactly what she—Sebastian—was doing.

Cesario spun on his heel and marched from the outpost library.

Viola took a moment to place the tree in its hiding spot. With more books on the shelves, the spot was a bit more secure than it had been. Once she returned, she would work on making a better hiding spot for the tree. If Duke Orsino was going to keep sending Sebastian off on errands, then she would need a safe place to stash the sapling. She couldn't tote it around all over the island.

She knelt before Curio and scratched his ruff. "Keep an eye on the sapling for me, all right?"

The bookwyrm gave a growling purr and flicked his tail, almost sarcastically.

That was as much agreement as she was going to get.

Stuffing her hands in her pockets, she forced herself into a leisurely, long-legged stroll. The gait didn't feel right, but hopefully the glamour smoothed the rough edges off so that she looked more like Sebastian.

When she stepped out of the outpost library, she blinked at the glare of the sun. The light seared hotter than she was used to in the green shade of the Court of Knowledge. Here, the sunlight danced on the rolling ocean waves, glared against the white stones of the buildings and the paths, and soaked into the sandy shores.

The town sprawled below the palace in tiers. Row upon row of homes and shops.

This mysterious Lady Olivia likely didn't live among the common fae in the town. Viola should look for some kind of manor house. How many nobles could there be on a small island like this?

Turning away from the village, she took the graveled path between the sea grass and the scrub trees as it meandered farther into the interior of the island.

Occasionally, paths branched off, leading to small, stone houses with the ubiquitous red tiled roofs. None of these appeared large enough to qualify as manors, so she strolled on by.

Finally, she reached a multi-story manor—white stone, of course—surrounded by large trees and fenced in by a thick hedge.

Holding her head high, she opened the gate, marched down the drive, and knocked on the front door.

A goblin with the nose and whiskers of some kind of rodent opened the door. "May I help you?"

"I am one of the new outpost librarians. I am stopping by to let everyone know that the new outpost library will be open in eleven days for all your knowledge needs." Viola gave a small bow. That sounded official, right? It would be a handy excuse to stop at every manor house. "Is your lord or lady in?"

"No, he isn't in, but I will let him know." The goblin nodded, then closed the door.

That ruled this manor out. Unless Lady Olivia was married to a lord or was his daughter? No one had said if Lady Olivia lived alone or if she had a family. How was Viola to know?

She continued traversing the island, stopping at every larger house she found. At each one, she gave her excuse that she was merely introducing herself. Well, introducing herself as Sebastian. She met a few of the local nobility, and some of them already seemed to know Sebastian. They seemed confused that she was giving them information that they already knew, and she quickly made her excuses.

By the time she arrived at the far side of the island, she was hotter and sweatier than she had been in years. She should have thought to bring water along. This heat reminded her of the dry, dusty farm where she had grown up, before her family had fled to the Fae Realm.

One last manor house perched on a bluff overlooking a sheltered cove. Some kind of bushes with blue, puffy flowers grew along the front of the manor house while a tree with pink flowers trailed branches down to the water's edge. A perfectly picturesque setting, as many were here in the Fae Realm.

Viola swiped at her sweaty hair—her mind torn as she felt both Sebastian's short hair and her own long strands—and marched up the graveled drive to the house. Would her glamour show up just as sweaty as she really was? A part of her hoped her glamour would look more professional. The other part worried that if she wasn't sweaty, the person opening the door might get suspicious. Which was ridiculous. Whoever opened that door would believe she was Sebastian since they had no reason to think otherwise.

With a deep breath, she knocked on the door.

A petite woman standing just over four feet tall with pink hair and glittering wings opened the door. As soon as she peered up at Viola, a sparkling smile creased her face. "Sebastian! You've returned! Olivia will be delighted to see you!"

The good news was that Viola had finally found the right place.

The bad news was that apparently Olivia knew Sebastian. Not just knew him but knew him so well that her servants welcomed Sebastian this warmly.

This was bad. This was very, very bad.

Yet Viola had no choice but to follow the pixie woman inside and, when directed, perch on a settee in a pink and blue sitting room.

While it might have been smarter to bolt, she couldn't leave. She had to deliver Duke Orsino's message.

How well did Lady Olivia know Sebastian? Would she see through the glamour?

Footsteps scuffed on the floorboards behind her, coming closer. The hair on the back of Viola's neck prickled as she sensed the person sneaking closer.

Viola hopped to her feet and whirled.

A fae woman stood there in a sweeping pink gown. Her dark, glossy curls gathered in a messy chignon at the back of her head, leaving several curls loose against her brown skin. She was leaning forward, a warm smile on her face, as if she had been about to wrap her arms around the person she thought was Sebastian.

At Viola's sudden movement, the woman jumped back, placing a hand on her chest. Her smile dropped only briefly before returning. "Sebastian. You're back. I've missed you."

She stepped forward again, and Viola dodged back.

I have someone I want you to meet. That had been one of the last things Sebastian said to her before they stepped through the Anywhere Door.

Apparently, Lady Olivia was that *someone*.

Viola was in trouble.

Should she just tell Lady Olivia? Drop the glamour and reveal that she was really Viola masquerading as Sebastian?

But Viola didn't know Olivia. Sure, Sebastian did. Very well, in fact.

This situation was complicated. Dangerous. If Viola made one wrong move, she might put Sebastian and the whole of the Court of Knowledge at risk, given she didn't even know what was going on.

Until Viola knew more, she couldn't risk telling anyone. Not even this Lady Olivia.

She would just have to make sure Lady Olivia didn't touch her or see beneath the glamour to realize that she wasn't the real Sebastian.

Viola dug into her pocket and pulled out the note from Duke Orsino. "I have a message from Duke—"

Lady Olivia cut her off with a groan and dropped onto the settee where Viola had been sitting moments ago. She pressed her hands to her face and groaned again. "He's turned you into his messenger boy now?"

Viola dropped the note onto the table and stepped back hurriedly before Lady Olivia could reach for her. "Yes, he asked me to take this to you and let you know that the outpost library has been established, as you requested."

Lady Olivia dropped her hands and peered up at her with deep brown eyes. "Don't sound so official, Sebastian. You know why I asked Favian to found an outpost library. We've been dreaming about this moment for years."

Wait, Lady Olivia and Sebastian had known each other for years? That was the reason for the outpost library?

If Olivia knew Sebastian that well, how long would it take her to see beneath the glamour?

Viola needed to get out of here as quickly as possible. She pointed to the note. "Aren't you going to read it? I need to tell Duke Orsino something."

"Read it? I know what it says." Olivia flopped back against the settee and flapped a hand toward the note. "It is filled with claims of love, but none of them are real. He no more loves me than I love him. But he is noble, and he loves this island. So he will keep that dratted bargain our fathers made no matter what, and call it love."

Bargain? What was Lady Olivia talking about? Bargains were serious things for the fae. If a bargain was involved, then this was something Viola would need to know.

Until she actually knew, she would need to pretend she knew so no one figured out she didn't know.

Olivia pinched the bridge of her nose, breaking the image of a perfectly put together fae lady. "Why hasn't he gotten the message by now? Can't he see that I'm avoiding him?"

"Why are you avoiding him?" Viola sank into the chair across the way.

Lady Olivia straightened, her gaze locking on Viola. "You know why, Sebastian. I can't marry him! I don't care about the bargain. I just care about marrying you!"

Viola blinked at the lady sitting across from her. It was as if she didn't even know Sebastian. He had been living a double life, keeping all these secrets even from Viola.

They never kept secrets from each other. Secrets were for Munch or Brigid, but not for Viola and Sebastian. They were almost like twins, sharing everything with each other. It was how they had survived those early years of drought.

Viola shook herself. Interrogating Sebastian would have to wait until after he was found safe and sound. Right now, she needed to keep pretending to be Sebastian, and she'd have to do such a great job of it that the glamour would hold up even under Lady Olivia's scrutiny.

It turned out it wasn't only Sebastian's job that she had to keep for him until he got back. She would have to keep up his romance as best she could until he returned.

She cleared her throat and forced out the words, trying to make them low and romantic. "I want to marry you too."

Ugh, this felt so wrong. Sebastian had better be safe and show up whole and healthy soon.

Olivia leaned forward, reaching as if expecting Sebastian to take her hand. "Have you found any way out of this bargain in your research at the Great Library?"

Viola couldn't take Olivia's hand, otherwise she would see beneath the glamour. Instead, she shook her head and heaved a sigh. "No."

She didn't know what Sebastian might have found during his secret research. Why wouldn't he have told her?

She would have helped. The entire family would have. No one knew the Great Library as well as Basil did. Their brother-in-law probably would have found the information in mere minutes.

But right now, it was safest to claim that she—Sebastian —had found nothing.

Olivia blinked, her eyes growing wet. She sprang from her seat, reaching for Viola. "Sebastian…"

Viola popped to her feet and dodged the fae woman's grasping fingers.

Olivia halted, a tear trickling down her face, as her forehead puckered. "Sebastian? What's wrong? You aren't acting like yourself."

The real Sebastian probably would have taken the woman he loved into his arms, embracing her. Apparently they had been carrying on a secret romance for years.

But Viola wasn't about to do that. There was only so far she would go in pretending to be her brother, no matter the whole glamour problem.

She would just need some excuse. There seemed to be some kind of bargain involving Lady Olivia and Duke Orsino, and Sebastian was trying to break it. That bargain must stand in the way of Sebastian and Lady Olivia being together.

"I'm sorry, but now that I'm here, I don't think it's a wise idea to get too close. What if Duke Orsino were to find out?" Viola backed toward the door. "And the bargain. It was risky enough when we were in two different courts. But now that I'm living on the island, crossing the bargain could get dangerous."

"I don't care, Sebastian! I can't take this anymore! We have to find a way out of this. I don't know how much longer I'll be able to put him off." Olivia reached for Viola again.

Viola dodged yet again, this time stumbling out the door into the hallway. "I'm sorry, Olivia, but I need to go. Please, don't try to find me at the outpost library. We need to be smart about this. Please."

Olivia nodded, her expression smoothing for the first time since this conversation started. "All right. But, please, don't leave me here alone. It would be torture, knowing you are here on the island, and I can't even see you."

Bother. The real Sebastian would probably sneak around to see Olivia. He had likely been doing just that for the past two years, ever since he started talking about founding an outpost library.

"I'll...I'll come back the day after tomorrow. After dark. We can meet in the garden."

Olivia smiled, the expression somehow both warm and sad. "Our usual spot then?"

Viola nodded. She would just have to make her best guess. She had already guessed right about meeting in the garden.

"I hoped our days of sneaking would be over, once you were here." Olivia rested a hand on the back of a chair, as if to steady herself.

"Me too." Viola forced herself to smile, then she turned and hurried for the door. Hopefully night would be cloak enough to keep the glamour in place.

It would be even better if Sebastian wandered out of the Anywhere Door and everything went back to normal.

Chapter Six

Before returning to the outpost library, Viola took a moment to check the Anywhere Door. It still wouldn't open.

Once back in the library, Viola changed back into herself and unpacked more books. Perhaps she should report to Duke Orsino first, but she needed to get something done to show for the day. The duke could wait, and she needed time to figure out what to tell him.

Clearly, Sebastian and Lady Olivia had been keeping their romance a secret, even from Duke Orsino. Until Viola knew more about the duke and this whole situation, she would have to keep that secret as well.

So many secrets. From Lady Olivia. From Duke Orsino.

She was just a simple librarian. All she was trying to do was save her brother's job until he returned from wherever he was. That was it. And suddenly she had found herself caught up in all of…this. Whatever *this* was.

As she set another stack of books on a shelf, bootsteps sounded against the stone floor. Moments later, Duke

Orsino paced around one of the shelves, taking in the books she'd already organized. A frown tugged his face into deeper lines. "Are you really going to put the references on magical talking animals next to the poetry?"

His tone bristled against her skin in a way that made her prickly. "This isn't the final organization. I can't see what I'm working with until I've unpacked all the boxes. Putting the books on the shelves in some semblance of order is better than making stacks on the ground where I would be tripping over them."

"Hmm." His grunt was just noncommittal enough that she couldn't tell if he was agreeing or not yet convinced and didn't want to admit it. "Has your brother returned?"

"No, not yet." Viola turned back to the nearest crate of books, keeping her back to the duke as she finished her lie. "I believe he planned to stop at all the noble houses and introduce himself."

If the duke were to ask, the nobles would tell him that Sebastian had stopped by. Sure, it hadn't taken all day, but she doubted the duke or the fae nobles would specify the time of day Sebastian had stopped by.

Duke Orsino remained silent long enough that Viola peeked over her shoulder at him. He regarded the shelves with that same frown.

Finally, he gave a nod and swung his gaze to her. "I'll wait."

Fiddlesticks. That was the last thing she was hoping he would say. How was she supposed to work—and think of a lie to tell him—if he kept glowering at the shelves for the rest of the day?

She drew up her shoulders, gathered all of her courage and sass, and turned to face the fae duke. "Since you have such vocal opinions on the organization of this outpost library, you could help me unpack, especially if you plan to stick around for the rest of the day."

Duke Orsino blinked down at her, his dour frown never wavering.

Viola dropped her gaze, gripping the book in her hand tighter. Perhaps she had been just a bit too snarky. She didn't know this fae duke. She probably should have kept her words a bit more respectful. Sure, she wasn't technically a part of Duke Orsino's court. And he couldn't exactly unceremoniously return her to the Court of Knowledge while the Anywhere Door wasn't working. But he could still make her life rather uncomfortable here if she offended him.

Duke Orsino's boots halted next to her, and he reached into the crate, pulling out a book. His gaze flicked over the title. "Where are the plays going?"

"I've been putting them on that shelf for now." Viola pointed to one of the highest shelves she could reach without pulling over one of the rolling ladders. She loved all the rolling ladders, of course. Especially the fact that the curving shelves meant that one ladder could service a long spiral of shelves. But climbing up and down the ladder each time she found another book for that section would be a lot of work while she was sorting the books.

Duke Orsino easily reached the shelf and slid the book into place. His expression didn't exactly waver, but did it soften? At least he didn't seem to be glowering so intently anymore. It was more like he had a resting frown face, and he didn't know how to undo the deep lines.

Viola handed him the book she was holding, then pointed at another shelf. "This one goes over there."

He obligingly shelved the book by the others that were similar.

Well, if he was truly going to help, then she wasn't going to argue. This was a huge job just for her, and it would be handy to have someone taller and stronger on hand.

That person was supposed to be Sebastian.

Viola swallowed and shoved that thought away. She couldn't think about Sebastian right now, not with Duke Orsino watching her. She forced a smile and dug through the crate, pulling out more books.

She and Duke Orsino fell into a steady rhythm of pulling out books, then shelving them with other similar books. It was strangely comfortable. Almost.

If only Sebastian was here. Then everything would be all right.

FAVIAN REACHED into the crate for another book, but his hand brushed Librarian Viola's fingers.

She jerked her hand away, her cheeks flushing a hint pink. Her slightly wavy blonde hair trailed down her back while a faint floral scent hung around her, subtle as the gray skirt and shirt she wore beneath her librarian's coat.

He cleared his throat, then picked up the book. It was another book on talking animals, and he didn't have to ask where it went. The few minutes it took to cross to the shelf and place the book next to the others gave him time to shake off the moment. Whatever kind of moment it had been.

She was a human librarian from another court. He had a bargain to fulfill. He couldn't let himself be attracted to anyone else besides Olivia. Not that he was attracted to Librarian Viola. He had merely noted, in the most logical manner possible, that she was attractive in a cute, human sort of way.

Some conversation would provide a distraction. It was only polite that he get to know the new librarians since they would be working closely together.

"What brought you to the Court of Knowledge?" Favian reached for another book. A history of one of the courts. He shelved it by the other histories. "It is unusual for humans to make their home in the Fae Realm, especially as full members of a court."

"My sister married a fae librarian." Viola glanced at him, shrugged, and turned back to the crate. "We had nothing to lose in the Human Realm, since our kingdom was suffering under a drought at the time, so when my sister and brother-in-law offered a home in the Court of Knowledge, with King Theseus's blessing, we decided we would rather make our home in the Fae Realm and stick together. We haven't regretted that decision. The Fae Realm is our home now."

Fascinating. He had heard of humans who had been snatched eventually falling in love with the Fae Realm and staying, even after their rescue.

But Viola and her family weren't snatched. Well, they were. But they weren't taken unwillingly as so many humans were. Their snatching was the willing kind of snatching.

"I'm glad you found a home in the Court of Knowledge." Favian checked another book and added it to a shelf. "I've heard King Theseus and Queen Hippolyta are honorable. They certainly seemed so in our negotiations for this outpost library."

Honor was a rare thing in a fae, much less a fae monarch. A few of the courts were ruled by good monarchs, like King Theseus. But more of them were ruled by kings or queens like King Oberon and Queen Titania of the Court of Revels. Real nutcases, those two. He'd only had the displeasure of meeting them once, and once was one time too many.

"They are." Viola added another book to a shelf. "I'm thankful Basil belongs to a Court with such honorable monarchs. That drought in our kingdom in the Human Realm was caused by a bad bargain a local duke made with an evil fae."

Favian grabbed another book, but he stared down at the title without really seeing it. "A bargain caused a drought over a whole kingdom?"

"Yes." Viola gave a slight shudder. She, too, stared down at a book and didn't seem to see it. "The fae was using the bargain to conduct blood rites, and he created the drought to force the lord to cooperate. Do you remember those three fae who caused trouble in the Court of Revels years ago? I wasn't in the Fae Realm at the time, but I've heard plenty of stories since. It was one of those three. My brother-in-law's older sister killed him."

Favian swallowed and forced himself to move. He had to check the title three times before he took it in enough to put the book on the proper shelf.

That was the consequence of a broken fae bargain. What kind of consequences would he face if he didn't fulfill the bargain to marry Lady Olivia? Sure, he didn't have an evil fae manipulating the bargain. But bargains had a way of destroying things along the way, even without outside manipulation.

How much of that drought had been caused by the evil fae and how much had the fae been using the natural magic of a broken bargain to his advantage?

He shook himself. "I am sorry you were caught up in the results of a fae bargain."

Viola peeked up at him, opened her mouth, then didn't speak, as if hesitating. After a moment, she met his gaze. "I've heard that you are also caught up in a bargain?"

He sighed and grabbed two more books, glancing at the titles. Of course Viola would have already heard about his bargain. It wasn't exactly a secret, and the whole island was freely gossiping about Olivia's refusal to so much as see him.

Favian tucked the books on a shelf, buying himself a few more seconds to gather his thoughts. "My father was good friends with Olivia's father, especially after both of our mothers died young and they were left to raise their young children as single fathers."

"That sounds like a tough childhood." Viola's tone lowered as she peered up at him.

"It wasn't all bad. Olivia and I are good friends. Or we were until our fathers were both killed in a shipwreck two years ago." Favian resisted the urge to drag his hand through his hair. He had actively worked to curb that impulse so that he didn't ruin his put together appearance as the lord of this island.

"I lost both of my parents as well. The grief never fully goes away, does it?" Viola shook her head as she sorted through a few more books. "They've missed so much of our lives. I wonder if they would be proud of who we've become. We're so different than the children we were back in the Human Realm."

"I'm sure they would be proud. As I know my parents would be of me." At least, Favian hoped they would be proud. He worked hard to be even half the lord his father had been. "Years ago, our fathers made a bargain that Lady Olivia and I would marry. It had been half in jest, but they made it a real, binding bargain shortly before they died."

"I see. That's tough. Bargains aren't to be messed with." Viola's voice held a note that he couldn't quite discern. She wasn't looking at him.

"No, they aren't." Favian stepped back, not reaching for another book. "Do you expect your brother will be back soon?"

What was taking so long? Surely Librarian Sebastian had spoken with Lady Olivia by now. The island wasn't that large. Even if he had taken the time to speak with all the nobles, they wouldn't linger over the conversation.

Viola hopped to her feet. "I'll check if he's back."

Before Favian could respond, she dashed around the corner, disappearing among the shelves.

Strange. If Sebastian was back, he would have come back here. There wasn't anything else to do in the outpost library. All the books were here in the crates.

But moments later, Sebastian strode around the shelves, brushing off his librarian coat. "I apologize for the delay. I was checking on the Anywhere Door."

"Any change?" Favian crossed his arms and faced the librarian.

"I'm afraid not." Sebastian shifted, not meeting Favian's gaze.

"And Olivia?" Favian struggled to keep his face blank and his tone even.

"She met with me. But…" Sebastian still wouldn't meet

Favian's gaze. "She still does not wish to see you. She wouldn't even read your note."

Favian clenched his fists. Why not? Where had he gone wrong with Olivia? They used to be such great friends. "Did she say why?"

Sebastian hesitated, then shook his head. "No."

There was something in that hesitation. As if Sebastian knew the answer but was unwilling to share it.

Favian gritted his teeth. He couldn't force Sebastian to tell him. Sebastian was not a part of his court. Even if Favian was willing to take more drastic measures, he did not think such a thing would be wise. He didn't want to add war with the Court of Knowledge to his list of problems if King Theseus found out Favian had bound or bargained or otherwise tampered with his librarian in any way.

Still, it was unutterably frustrating. What was this big secret that made Olivia avoid him and Librarian Sebastian keep his mouth shut?

Why wouldn't they trust him? Was there something wrong with Favian that those closest to him felt compelled to keep secrets from him?

Chapter Seven

The next morning, Favian struggled to concentrate on his stacks of paperwork. The light, summer breezes blew in the scent of the sea and warm sand, making it hard to remain indoors on a day like this.

After pretending to work for a few more minutes, he finally pushed away from his desk. The day was simply too nice, and he was too restless to actually accomplish anything.

As he stood, Cesario hopped to his feet as well, standing behind the smaller, sprite-sized desk tucked into a corner. "Is there something you need, my lord?"

"I'm going to be out for a while." Favian strode past the sprite quickly enough so that he didn't catch his steward's expression. Not that it mattered. Even if Cesario judged him for skiving off like he was still a child instead of the duke of the island, the sprite would never let his thoughts show on his face.

Favian took the nearest double doors onto the broad porch, the tension in his shoulders relaxing as he leisurely strolled the length of the porch. The sea breeze ruffled his hair, bringing with it the faint sounds of the bustling town below.

This was his island. To rule. To protect. Even if that meant honoring a bargain made by his late father.

Even as he thought it, he found his feet heading in the direction of the outpost library. Perhaps thoughts of Olivia drew him to see to it that her dream of an outpost library became a reality.

The sea breezes followed him inside the outpost library. All the windows were cranked open, their gauzy curtains blowing in and out.

A blue bookwyrm glanced at him as he closed the door before scurrying off into the maze of shelves. Otherwise, the outpost appeared deserted.

Where were the librarians? Shouldn't they be bustling about in here? It wasn't like they could return to the Court of Knowledge since the Anywhere Door currently wasn't working.

Favian followed the curving pathways between the shelves until he reached the far back corner.

Here the top of a golden head was barely visible behind stacks and stacks of books. It appeared that since he left yesterday, Viola and her brother had unpacked the rest of the crates. They must have given up on putting books on shelves temporarily, for books were piled on the floor, leaving only little walkways between them.

"Librarian Viola?" Favian halted, eyeing the two book-wyrms that were curled in front of a basket containing a sapling. The two bookwyrms blinked slitted eyes right back at him, their ruffs puffing out slightly. Not menacing but still alert and warning.

Viola gave a little squeak, then stumbled. She tumbled over, a whole stack of books tumbling with her.

Favian peered around the books, trying to make sure the petite librarian hadn't been buried under a book avalanche. "Are you all right, Librarian Viola?"

Viola sprawled on the flagstones, books piled on her lap and scattered all around her. A bookwyrm slithered through the carnage and nudged Viola with its nose.

"I'm fine." She pushed upright, swiping a strand of hair from her face, before she peered up at him. "What are you doing here, my lord?"

Favian eased between the piles of books, then picked up one of the scattered tomes from the floor. "I wished to see the progress of the outpost library."

Her chin jutted as her eyes flashed a bit. But she turned away from him as she, too, began plucking books from the floor. "It has been less than a day since you were last here. And there are only two of us."

There were two librarians, but he had yet to see Sebastian that morning. Why was it that he always seemed to leave his sister to do all the heavy lifting?

It wasn't Favian's place to question. While he was providing the outpost library, these librarians were under the authority of their librarian king.

But Favian wasn't going to stand by and watch while Viola struggled with all these books herself.

He knelt and reached for a few more books. "Would you like some help?"

She froze, her hand stilling on the book she had been about to pick up. Her shoulders rose and fell, as if in a steadying breath. But when she turned to him, she gave him a bright smile. "That would be really helpful. I was just sorting the last of the books, and I was about to haul the books to their places on the shelves." Her smile grew even brighter, dancing in her blue eyes. "Actually, since you love organization so much, would you like to help me decide how to lay out the sections of books?"

Now that did sound like an interesting way to spend his time. "I do believe I would enjoy that."

Her eyebrows shot up at his quick agreement. But then she pushed to her feet, set her books on a few shelves, then gestured to the rest of the library. "All right. Let's get started."

Favian followed her into the rest of the library, not sure why an eagerness filled his stride. "Is there a standard organization method that you learned in the Great Library?"

"Organization? Somewhat. Standard? Not really." Viola shrugged. "This is the Fae Realm, after all. The Great Library is divided into wings and sections. But it's sprawling, and each Head Librarian has his own way of doing things so organization is more based on their tastes and the Library's moods than anything else."

Hmm. That still sounded a bit haphazard for his taste. Favian pointed toward the main door. "I think the reference section should go up front. Those are the most important books."

Viola halted and planted her hands on her hips. "Reference books are no more and no less important than story books or poetry or any of those genres."

"They are more useful." Favian shrugged. He wasn't sure why she was arguing this point. The answer was obvious. Poetry and fluffy stories had their place, but they did not contain anything like the important information in nonfiction.

Viola just rolled her eyes and mumbled under her breath, "Maybe that's why Lady Olivia won't see you."

Favian stilled. Was that why Olivia found his notes lacking? "Is that the reason? You truly think Lady Olivia won't see me because I don't write her poetry or other frilly notes?"

Viola's gaze shot to him, and she pressed her hands to her mouth, as if she hadn't realized she'd said that loud enough that he could hear it. "I'm sorry. I shouldn't have said that. I forgot I couldn't just talk to myself."

Favian waved her protests away. Perhaps it had been impertinent, but she wasn't under his authority. She was free to voice her opinions. "I appreciate your insight. Perhaps you could provide me with a book of poetry once we are finished?"

"Of course, my lord. Providing the right book is my job." Viola gave a little curtsy, as if to make up for her earlier impertinence with formality now. She turned back to the front of the library. "Perhaps you do have a point. Maybe that curving shelf by the front can start with books about the Court of Islands, and the island of Melyria in particular, and flow into other informational books along that spiral."

"That sounds logical." Favian gave a slight nod.

Viola's smile returned as she gestured to the rest of the library, outlining her various plans for how to organize the space.

Favian occasionally broke in with objections, more to tease her than because he truly objected to the plan. All the while, he didn't let himself examine too closely the way her bright smile and sparkling eyes made him feel.

VIOLA FACED the piles upon piles of books waiting on the floor along with the rows upon rows of books on the surrounding shelves in the back corner. Planning out the library with Duke Orsino had been unexpectedly fun, once she figured out that most of his dour critiques were actually his way of teasing her. Who knew that the perpetually frowning lord actually had a sense of humor? If he actually smiled, he might appear more like the young fae lord he was.

But now the hard part started. Hauling all these books to their assigned places on the shelves.

As jumpy as his presence made her, she was grateful that Duke Orsino was here, especially for this part. As long as he didn't ask where Sebastian was.

Duke Orsino halted next to her and swept the explosion of books with that dour gaze and deep frown. Giving a slight nod, as if coming to some kind of decision, he shrugged out of his coat and laid it over one of the empty crates, giving a seemingly absent pat to the bookwyrm —Toby—curled there.

Viola couldn't help but gape a bit as he rolled up first one sleeve, then the other. There was just something trans-formative about those sleeves rolled up to his elbows. With his coat and sleeves down, he was the all-too-frowny fae lord. But with his coat off, his sleeves rolled up, and his hair tousled from the breezes coming through the windows, he looked young and handsome and like he might just smile at any moment if given the right incentive.

She shook herself. What was she thinking? Duke Orsino was a fae lord. He wasn't even a part of her court. Not to mention that he intended to marry Lady Olivia to fulfill a bargain.

Things were already confusing enough without Viola letting herself get attracted to a fae lord who needed to marry someone else.

Someone else who happened to be in love with her brother. A brother who was currently missing and whom Viola was impersonating.

Duke Orsino had turned to her, his frown currently looking more puzzled than disapproving. "Where would you like to begin?"

She hurriedly turned to the nearest stack of books and picked up the top half of the stack. Only once she had hefted them in her arms did she take a moment to take in the titles. Some of the reference books Duke Orsino loved so much. Not that she had anything against reference books. She loved all books. But she wasn't going to admit it to Duke Orsino.

He picked up the rest of the stack, then they navigated through the outpost until they reached the section designated for those books.

She plunked her books on the shelves. Once she got the books all in their sections, she would rearrange them to be alphabetical and stuff like that.

Together, she and Duke Orsino hauled the books to the different shelves all around the outpost library. While she was hauling the poetry books, she slipped one into her pocket to give to Duke Orsino later.

As Viola placed the last book on the shelves, she swiped the back of her hand over her sweaty forehead, dragging at the wisps of hair sticking to the sweat. She had ditched her librarian coat, thankful she had gone for an airy cornflower sundress underneath. While the Court of Knowledge was perpetually warm as a Summer Court, this island was far warmer.

Duke Orsino halted next to her, his hair even more tousled than before. Yet he still looked far less disheveled than she felt. "I believe that is the last one."

"Finally." Her arms ached, and she turned to the back of the library with a sigh. "I suppose I should break down the crates next."

Duke Orsino waved a hand. "I can send someone to help with the crates. Or your brother can tackle them when he returns."

It was the closest he had come all day to questioning where Sebastian was.

Viola didn't dare protest, otherwise he might question further. "Sebastian won't mind taking care of them. Thank you for all your help today."

He nodded, hesitating as if he wasn't ready to leave. Then he shifted, half-turning toward the door. "I should get back to my paperwork and leave you to continue organizing."

"Before you go, here's the poetry book you requested." Viola pulled it out of her pocket and held it out to him.

"Is this an official librarian recommendation?" Duke Orsino took it from her, something glinting in his eyes even if the frown lines remained etched deep around his mouth.

"Yes." She tried to sound confident. It wasn't like this was the first time she had recommended a book to someone in her job as a librarian. But this time felt a bit more momentous, somehow. Perhaps because there was no Sebastian to agree with her that she had made the right selection. No Basil to help her find the perfect book. No Head Librarian Marco to deal with complaints if she got it wrong. "This poet is regarded as one of the best classical poets of the Fae Realm."

"Then I shall endeavor to enjoy it." Duke Orsino gave her a hint of a bow before he turned on his heel and marched from the library.

Viola released her breath in a whoosh and braced herself against the nearest bookshelf. She wasn't even sure why her knees were a bit weak.

It had to be all the books she'd moved that day. They had been rather heavy, after all. No one would judge if she took a few minutes to sit and rest her aching feet.

That was all this feeling was. Just exhaustion.

Chapter Eight

Sebastian crawled inch by painful inch over the tilting, whirling ground between the realms. Each moment, it took all his concentration to hold on to the pieces of himself so that he wasn't pulled apart and scattered to all corners of the void.

His fingers brushed something. A flash of red arrested his failing senses.

He worked to peel his eyelids open wider, then he fought the forces pinning him to raise his head to peer at the blossom caught between his stretching fingers.

A tiny red flower. Pimpernel as it was called in the Human Realm. Wild fae primrose in the Fae Realm. The flower was his sister Brigid's symbol in her work as rescuer of kidnapped humans and fae alike.

There was a reason she had chosen this particular flower as her symbol. Sebastian squeezed his eyes shut, trying to get his swirling head to concentrate. There was something about the wild fae primrose…

It grew around faerie circles. And it was said that the flower led wanderers home.

He was a wanderer. And he certainly needed help finding his way home.

Plucking the flower, he strained to peer into the foggy whirl around him.

There. Another flash of red.

Sebastian dragged himself forward, his lungs aching as he struggled to draw in breath in this place. Was he breathing? Or was he so caught in the nothingness that he needed neither air nor food to simply exist? Or not exist, as the case might be?

He kept his eyes locked on the next dot of red and belly-crawled onward until he reached it.

No matter how long it took, he had to follow these flowers and find his way home. Too many people depended on him. He wasn't ready to lose his family or for them to lose him.

Then there was Olivia. No one even knew he had fallen in love. He wanted to introduce her to his family. To save her from her forced marriage to Duke Orsino. To build a life in the Fae Realm like his older sisters had.

He couldn't die here. He had to survive, no matter what it took.

AFTER ENJOYING Duke Orsino's help moving all the books, Viola changed into her Sebastian glamour to break up the crates. One of the duke's servants came to help. Luckily, the sprite likely didn't know enough about humans to find it odd that Viola was carrying far less than a man of Sebastian's size and strength would have been able to hold.

The next day, she spent most of the morning and into the afternoon organizing the books to their proper order on the shelves and familiarizing herself with each and every book in the place so that she could easily find something when someone asked.

She swapped back and forth between herself and her Sebastian glamour several times so that when Duke Orsino and a few of his servants stopped by to check on the outpost, Sebastian could make an appearance.

Once it was fully dark, she changed into her Sebastian glamour and set out on the hike across the island. It didn't take her as long now that she knew which manor house belonged to Lady Olivia, and she was able to arrive an hour before midnight.

It took some time of sneaking through the gardens before she found a bench tucked in the far back of the garden beneath an arbor with a fountain bubbling nearby.

This would be Olivia and Sebastian's usual spot, if Viola knew her brother as well as she thought she did. It was, also, the most secluded spot in the entire garden, perfect for a clandestine romance.

Since she wasn't actually Sebastian, she didn't wait on the bench but stood to one side of the arbor, out of sight in the shadows.

She didn't have to wait long before a figure hurried around the hedge, her skirts rustling in the darkness. "Sebastian?"

Viola didn't move from her hidden position. "Here."

Nothing but a blur of dark cloak, Olivia hurried forward and slid onto the bench, leaving plenty of space for a person to sit beside her. "Sebastian? Aren't you going to sit with me?"

"I think it would be best if I didn't." Viola eased a little deeper into the greenery of the arbor to keep it between herself and Olivia.

"I hate this." Olivia swiveled on the bench as if trying to face Sebastian in the darkness. She clenched her fists in her skirt, her expression shadowed. "Everything was supposed to be different when you arrived."

"I know. But until we can find a way to end the bargain safely, we can't let Duke Orsino know." Viola hoped her word choice sounded like something Sebastian would say. Of everyone on the island, Olivia had the most potential to see through the glamour.

Should Viola simply tell Olivia that Sebastian was missing? If Sebastian loved this fae lady, then surely she was trustworthy. It was cruel to keep up the glamour and not tell her that Sebastian was missing. It wasn't like Olivia was even talking to Duke Orsino right now, so he wouldn't find out even if Lady Olivia knew the truth. The outpost library and Sebastian's position in it would remain secure.

Would Duke Orsino toss her out if he knew she was all alone here? She'd thought so at first, but after spending so much time with him the past few days, she no longer believed that was the case. Perhaps she should tell him the truth as well and be done with the whole glamour.

"I might know of a way to end the bargain." Olivia fidgeted with her skirt. "I met someone today who claims to know how to end it."

Viola stilled. If they broke the bargain now, then Olivia would want to marry Sebastian right away. Viola would have to tell her the truth. "Did this person say how?"

"No, not yet. And I'm not sure how much I should trust him. He claims he is here to court me, and he says he can end the bargain so that he and I can marry." Olivia sighed and curled a bit tighter on herself. "That wouldn't solve our problem at all. But maybe if I pretend to let him court me, I can get him to tell me how to end the bargain."

"That sounds risky." Viola wasn't sure what to tell Lady Olivia. The fae lady sounded desperate to end the bargain forcing her to marry Duke Orsino. Would Sebastian want Viola to tell Olivia to risk it so that they could be together? Or would he tell her that he would rather she stayed safe and they would figure something else out?

"Any risk is worth it so that we can be together." Olivia reached out toward the darkness, as if hoping Sebastian would step out of the shadows to hold her.

If Sebastian was here, that was probably exactly what he would do. He would sit on that bench, pull Olivia into his arms, and murmur sweet nothings into her ear until he kissed her.

Viola shook her head. Imaging her brother kissing anyone was just…no. Nope, not doing it.

But she was here right now, pretending to be Sebastian, and she couldn't let Olivia think that Sebastian no longer loved her.

With this other fae lord in the picture, Viola couldn't tell Olivia the truth just yet. There was something suspicious about him showing up, claiming to know a way out of the bargain.

"Be careful. Whatever this fae lord has to say, it isn't worth risking yourself or Duke Orsino finding out that you are trying to end the bargain." Viola pressed a hand to the arbor. "I've been searching for a way out of the bargain. I'm sure I'll be able to find a way out in the Great Library if given a little more time."

Sebastian had likely already found a way out of the bargain. It was probably why he had promised Olivia that things would be different once he returned to the island, and he'd been so excited to introduce Viola to Olivia. Sebastian had believed that he had a way out.

All Viola had to do was stall Olivia until Sebastian returned, then Sebastian could straighten all of this out.

"Who is this fae lord? Is he someone from one of the other islands?" Viola shifted from foot to foot. It would have been so much nicer to sit for this conversation. She'd been on her feet all day working in the outpost library.

But she couldn't get close to Olivia or she'd risk that Olivia would touch her and see beneath the glamour.

Olivia stilled, then smoothed her hands over her skirts. "Lord Chauvlyn of the Court of Revels."

Viola froze, her stomach sinking. Not only was Lord Chauvlyn working with King Oberon of the Court of Revels, but he was also associated with Claudius, one of three evil fae who had been banished from the Fae Realm.

Viola found herself stepping forward before she halted herself. "Don't trust him, Olivia. He's dangerous."

"I know. You've warned me about him. But I'm sure he won't risk angering the Court of Islands by hurting a lady of the islands." Olivia was too oblivious. Too trusting.

"He briefly captured my sister, a member of the Court of Knowledge. We've been on the brink of war with the Court of Revels for two years because of his actions." Viola clenched her fists, her heart racing. "If he's here, then he's up to no good. You can't trust anything he says. I don't think he has a way to end the bargain. Or if he does, he will just trap you into a worse bargain."

What was he doing here? Lord Chauvlyn didn't do things just for the fun of it. If he was here, then it was part of some kind of plot.

Whether that plot was his, King Oberon's, or Claudius's remained to be seen. But one thing was certain, he wasn't here just to court Olivia. That was just an excuse. A cloak to hide his real intentions.

It couldn't be a coincidence that he was here on this island the moment the Anywhere Doors stopped working and the outpost library was supposed to be founded. It must be all tied together somehow.

Olivia leaned forward. "All the more reason I have to pretend to allow him court me. I can't let him know I'm suspicious. Maybe he doesn't have the answer to ending the bargain. But perhaps I can figure out his real reason for being here. It seems suspicious that he would show up here so soon after your arrival, given his connection to your sister Brigid."

Olivia might be naïve, but she wasn't unintelligent. She had seen the same thing Viola had, and she didn't even know Lord Chauvlyn the way Viola and Sebastian did.

Viola had been tempted to tell Olivia the truth that Sebastian was missing, but now she definitely couldn't. She couldn't breathe a word of the truth to anyone. It was imperative Lord Chauvlyn believed that the outpost library was staffed by both Sebastian and Viola. Who knew what he would do if he realized Viola was here alone.

A cold dread washed over her. Could Lord Chauvlyn harm the sapling? It was tucked in its hiding spot, but the hiding spot was only to prevent a casual rabble rouser from stumbling over the tree. It wouldn't take Lord Chauvlyn long to discover it if he had the chance to search the outpost library.

"Please stay away from Lord Chauvlyn as much as you can, Olivia. Please." Viola backed away from the arbor, itching to run. "I need to return to the outpost library. I can't leave the…I can't leave Viola alone if Lord Chauvlyn is on the island."

"Of course. I understand." Olivia stood as well, moving as if to reach for the person she thought was Sebastian.

Viola did the only thing she could think to do.

She ran.

She didn't stop until she was well away from Lady Olivia's manor house, and she was forced to slow because she was panting too hard to keep up the pace.

Once she had caught her breath, she jogged and walked the entire way across the island back to the outpost library.

The outpost library's door was locked, but that didn't mean anything. Lord Chauvlyn no doubt could pick a lock just as well as Brigid could.

Viola opened the door with the key, then stepped inside. The lamps by the door flared to life, though shadows still clung to the spiraling maze of shelves. Any number of dangers could lurk, waiting to snatch her.

Until the sapling could be planted and grow into an extension of the Great Library's tree, this building was just a shell. It wasn't warm and protective and comforting the way the Great Library was back home. Here dangers could lurk and the library wouldn't step in to protect her.

Viola straightened her shoulders and, heart pounding in her throat, made her way through the shelves.

As she navigated around one of the curving turns, something moved in the shadows up ahead, rasping and casting a long, dark shadow.

Viola jumped and reached into the pocket of her librarian coat for her club. Was it a monster that had come through a rift from the Realm of Monsters? Lord Chauvlyn come to snatch her?

Curio slithered out of the shadows, his ruff relaxed. He wound around her feet, making the growling noises that passed as a bookwyrm purr.

Viola released a breath, trying to still her pounding heart. Just one of the bookwyrms. Nothing to get all jumpy about.

When she finally reached the back corner, all four book-wyrms gathered around her as she pulled the sapling from its hiding spot.

The sapling was fine. The library was empty except for her and the four bookwyrms. She didn't have anything to be afraid of.

Tonight, anyway. Tomorrow she would have to figure out what to do about this new danger.

Lord Chauvlyn was dangerous, and it was imperative that he believed there were two librarians guarding this library, not just one girl trying to be two people and armed with nothing besides a glamour necklace and her wits.

Chapter Nine

Favian neatly stacked his finished paperwork on a corner of his desk, ready for Cesario to either file or to distribute to the recipients. After ditching his responsibilities the other day, it was all the more satisfying to be caught up.

So caught up, that perhaps he could justify taking another afternoon to spend with Librarian Viola.

He couldn't help but glance at the book of poetry he'd set on the corner of his desk. Or, maybe, he would read a few of the poems before he wandered to the outpost library. Librarian Viola was bound to ask him about the book, and he wouldn't want to admit that he had yet to bring himself to crack it open.

A sharp rap sounded on the door a moment before Cesario stepped inside, all three feet of him standing short and proper in a dark blue doublet and trousers that nearly matched the color of his hair. "Librarian Sebastian is here to see you, my lord."

Interesting. The elusive Librarian Sebastian. What brought him to Favian's study this early in the morning?

Not that Favian minded. He would like a discussion of his own with the librarian. Namely, why he kept disappearing and leaving his sister with so much work.

"Send him in." Favian glanced over his desk, checking that it was indeed pristine. His gaze caught on the book of poetry again, and he quickly snatched it from the desk.

He wasn't sure why he felt so compelled to hide the book. Librarian Viola had likely told her brother that she had helped find a book for the island's duke. Was there such a thing as librarian-patron confidentiality? All the same, he wasn't ready to let this particular librarian see the book.

Cesario stepped back out, holding the door open. "You may enter, Librarian Sebastian."

Sebastian strolled inside, wearing his black librarian coat, and carrying a basket with a sapling inside. One of the bookwyrms peeked over the edge of the basket, a pink, forked tongue flicking in and out as the wyrm peered around.

Sebastian gave a hint of a bow to Favian. "Duke Orsino. Thank you for taking the time to speak with me."

There was something grave in the librarian's voice that set Favian's skin to prickling, making his lecture about leaving Viola all by herself dying on his lips.

But he kept his expression blank as he motioned to a chair with his free hand. With his other, he was carefully sliding open one of the desk drawers, doing it slowly so that he neither made noise nor appeared to be moving. "Please, have a seat. What brings you here?"

Sebastian sat, then set the basket on his lap, cradling it to his chest almost like the sapling was as precious as a child. He drew in a deep breath, his shoulders rising and falling, before he met Favian's gaze. "I called on Lady Olivia again to see if she had reconsidered and wished to reply to your note."

Favian slid the poetry book into the drawer and slowly eased it shut. That was good initiative on the librarian's part. Though it rankled that Olivia seemed willing to talk with this librarian when she refused to so much as answer Favian's note. "Did she have a reply?"

"No." Sebastian's gaze dropped, and his fingers flexed on the basket. "But what she did have to say was worrisome enough that I thought I should come to you. Lord Chauvlyn of the Court of Revels is here on the Island of Melyria, and he is attempting to court Lady Olivia, despite the bargain your fathers had."

Favian braced his hands on his desk, his stomach sinking. What else could go wrong? First the Anywhere Doors, now the Court of Revels meddling in his affairs. "Does he know she is part of a bargain?"

"Yes, though he claims he has a way to end the bargain so that Lady Olivia would be free to marry him instead. Lady Olivia is, understandably, wary of him." Librarian Sebastian met Favian's gaze again, his blue eyes sharp. "You, too, should be wary, Duke Orsino. As you might know, my family has a history with Lord Chauvlyn. I highly doubt Lord Chauvlyn is here to court Lady Olivia. I worry that his appearance on the island might have more to do with the outpost library, given his court's current animosity toward the Court of Knowledge. That's why I thought it best to warn you and beg for your cooperation to secure the outpost while Lord Chauvlyn is on the island."

Favian leaned back in his chair and steepled his fingers. "You did right in coming to me."

While Favian didn't know the whole story of what had happened between Lord Chauvlyn and Librarian Sebastian's family, he had known of the animosity between the two courts. It was hard not to know, when the Court of Knowledge had taken the drastic step of barring the Court of Revels from using the Anywhere Doors.

By creating the outpost library, Favian had aligned himself with the Court of Knowledge. It wasn't a close alliance, but there was language in the agreement between him and King Theseus that amounted to the same thing.

When it came down to it, Favian wasn't in favor of the capture of humans. Or the trade of capturing the lesser fae to sell to humans. That put Favian more on the side of King Theseus and the fae hero the Wild Fae Primrose than on the side of Lord Chauvlyn and the Court of Revels.

"I will see to it that additional guards are stationed around the outpost library." Favian eyed Librarian Sebastian, an odd tension filling his stomach at the thought that Librarian Viola was in the outpost library right now, alone, unguarded. "Would you and your sister feel safer if you had a guard escort whenever you leave the outpost?"

Librarian Sebastian hesitated, a strange expression flashing in his eyes for a moment, before he shook his head. "I don't believe that will be necessary, at least not all the time. But if either of us feel the need for an escort, would we be able to make a request then?"

Favian nodded. With guards stationed both around the outpost library and on the porch of the palace facing the outpost, the librarians would be in sight of guards the entire walk from the palace to the outpost. "I will alert my guards to assist if such a request is made by either you or Librarian Viola."

"Thank you. I appreciate your help in securing the outpost library." Sebastian tipped his head in a nod. "I'm sure King Theseus will express his appreciation as well once the Anywhere Doors are working again."

While King Theseus's appreciation was gratifying, Favian wasn't being so cooperative for the sake of the agreement.

Favian wasn't sure he wanted to examine his real reasons too closely. It wasn't Olivia's face and her dream of an outpost library that popped into his mind.

But Viola, sitting on the floor surrounded by books. Viola, as she handed him a book of poetry. Viola, kneeling to pet a bookwyrm.

Favian shook his head. Librarian Viola shouldn't fill his thoughts so much, especially since he had only known her a handful of days.

Olivia was the lady he would marry, and he had no choice in the matter.

This was just a passing feeling. He was sure once he figured out what was going on with Olivia, things would go back to the way they were. Whatever draw he felt to Librarian Viola would fade away because it surely couldn't be a solid thing after only a few days' time.

"Thank you for bringing me this information. If that is all, perhaps you should return to the outpost library to help Viola guard it until my guards arrive." Favian waved in dismissal, staying in his chair by sheer willpower when everything in him wanted to leap to his feet and ensure Viola's safety in person.

But that wouldn't be the action of a composed duke. So

he stayed where he was.

Sebastian popped to his feet, gave another bow while still gripping the basket, mumbled something unintelligible, and hurried out the door.

"Cesario!" Favian reached for a sheet of paper, writing out his instructions.

"Yes, my lord?" Cesario bounded inside, halting before Favian's desk.

"Carry these instructions to the head of my guards. I want a constant guard rotation to keep the outpost library and the librarians safe." Favian folded that piece of paper, then reached for a second paper, scribbling out more instructions. "I also want Lord Chauvlyn located and put under surveillance. But be discreet and cautious. We don't want him to know he is under watch, nor do we wish to start an incident with the Court of Revels. But I want to know his whereabouts at all times."

"Yes, my lord." Cesario's expression never wavered to betray what he thought about such instructions.

Favian folded the second message, then sealed both. He handed them to Cesario.

Cesario bowed. "I will see that these are delivered posthaste, my lord."

As the sprite hurried away, Favian remained where he was, staring at his desk for a long moment.

It was indeed worrisome that a lord from the Court of Revels was here, right when the outpost library was being founded and the Anywhere Doors weren't working for some mysterious reason.

How much should Favian get involved? Politically, the Court of Islands was neutral in this little tiff between the Court of Revels and Court of Knowledge. As a lord of the

Court of Islands, Favian wasn't supposed to do anything that would support one side or the other.

In practicality, the Court of Islands was much less politically united than the other courts. Each duke was given freer rein to decide the political affiliations of his particular island or islands. If Favian took a stand on one side or the other, it wouldn't necessarily drag the whole Court of Islands into it.

But Favian would be alone. It would be his island against one side or the other.

Assuming the tiff spilled over into something more than just the cold standoff that the two courts had been experiencing for the past few years.

Did Favian really have a choice? If Lord Chauvlyn made any kind of move against the outpost library, Favian would be obligated to step in to uphold the agreement—tantamount to a bargain—that he had with King Theseus regarding the library and its librarians.

Not only that, but Lord Chauvlyn was ostensibly here to court Lady Olivia. Just that alone jeopardized Favian's island. Especially since Favian found Lord Chauvlyn's claim to be able to end the bargain dubious at best.

Perhaps that was the point? Lord Chauvlyn intended to lure Olivia into breaking the bargain in the worst way possible, unleashing the destructive magic of an unkept bargain on the island.

For what purpose? Just to cause chaos? Why would Lord Chauvlyn and King Oberon target Favian's little island? He was hardly the most wealthy of dukes, nor did he lead the largest of islands. He didn't even rule over multiple islands the way some of the more powerful dukes did.

Favian shook himself. The truth was that he did not have

enough information yet to do more than uselessly speculate. He knew to be wary, and he had taken all the logical steps he could. Until his surveillance of Lord Chauvlyn yielded results, Favian would simply have to continue to be cautious.

What he could do was step up his attempts to talk to Olivia. He could at least ensure that Olivia wouldn't do anything foolish, like take Lord Chauvlyn up on his offer.

Glancing around the study, Favian opened the drawer and pulled out the book of poetry. It was time to stop delaying and start reading.

He flipped to the first page.

Living, I die
Dying, living
Nothing, nothing
Everything
Gone

Favian couldn't help the curl to his mouth as he contemplated the poem. What in all the Fae Realm had he just read? Was this considered literature?

He forged ahead through several more poems but each one was more puzzling than the last.

Was he supposed to get something out of this? If he should get some kind of emotion out of this, then he wasn't seeing it. He definitely wasn't seeing how reading these poems would help him with Lady Olivia.

Perhaps he should consult with Librarian Viola. She was the one who had recommended the book, after all. And he really ought to see for himself that the guards were in place, as he had ordered.

A convenient excuse. But he wasn't going to argue with himself over it.

Tucking the book in an inner pocket of his coat where his guards wouldn't see it, Favian pushed to his feet and let that allure carry him in the direction of the outpost library.

As soon as she returned to the outpost library, Viola dropped the Sebastian glamour and set to work organizing the books. She hadn't been satisfied with the flow of the original arrangement, so she was switching books to different shelves.

She set the basket with the sapling where she could keep it in sight while she moved between the shelves. Feste and Toby remained by the basket, watching the sapling and her in turns, while Curio and Belch disappeared among the shelves. Hunting, or possibly keeping watch in their own bookwyrm kind of way.

She kept a wary eye out of the window, and shortly after she returned, four fae dressed in chainmail vests and carrying swords took up positions around the outpost.

The sight of the guards helped her breathe a little easier, but the guards likely wouldn't be able to truly stop Lord Chauvlyn if he wanted to try something. He was too crafty.

But at least Duke Orsino knew to be wary, and steps were being taken to protect the outpost library.

Viola fell into a rhythm of moving stacks of books, organizing them back into order, and going for more.

As she rounded the corner with another armload of books, she came face to face with a figure coming toward her. She nearly rammed her stack of books into his chest as she halted abruptly.

Duke Orsino reached out a hand and steadied the stack

of books. "I thought you were done with putting the books on the shelves."

Viola glared down at Curio by Duke Orsino's feet. Apparently the duke was becoming such a fixture of the outpost library that the bookwyrms hadn't even bothered to alert her to the duke's presence.

"We were. But I didn't like the organization. So I'm moving a few things." Viola forced a smile, though she couldn't quite bring herself to meet the duke's gaze. Would he be offended that she was changing the system that the two of them had worked on together?

Instead of being offended, the barest hint of a smile creased the corners of his mouth. "I told you that putting the medical texts by the biography tomes would never do."

Fiddlesticks, but he had told her that.

Yet that hint of a smile was teasing, a glimpse of a sense of humor that she never would have guessed he possessed when she first met him.

"I would bow to your superior sense of organization, but my arms are too full of books." Her forced smile relaxed into something real as she juggled the armload.

"Allow me." Duke Orsino took the stack from her.

If the duke had been Sebastian, she would have protested that she was perfectly capable of carrying the books by herself.

But it felt different when the duke offered to carry the books for her. Perhaps because Sebastian never would even think to carry the books for her since he knew Viola's capabilities. And he was her brother. That was different.

"I'm bringing them over here." Viola led the way around the shelves until she reached the new section.

Duke Orsino placed the books on the shelves, then stood back while she quickly put the books into proper order.

Once she was finished, she turned back to the duke. "What brings you to the outpost library today?"

Duke Orsino scratched the back of his neck, shifting a bit. "I confess, I've been struggling to make sense of that book of poetry you gave me. I don't believe poetry is to my taste."

Viola worked to put a stricken look on her face. "Oh. That was my favorite."

Duke Orsino gave a small cough. "I...that is to say, I don't think the poetry is bad. I am sure they are very lovely poems."

She couldn't keep the look in place a moment longer and gave in to the urge to grin.

"Ah." Duke Orsino gave her that lopsided attempt at a smile. "I see. You are putting me on."

"Oh, most definitely." Viola shook her head, still grinning. "You clearly didn't grow up with siblings."

"No, though Olivia was much like a sister." Duke Orsino trailed off, the smile disappearing as his gaze went unfocused, staring past Viola's head. Then he shook himself and pulled the poetry book from his pocket. "Is there another book of poems that would be more to my taste than this one?"

"Perhaps. Let's see." Viola motioned for him to follow her to the poetry section. There, she picked several books off the shelves. "Why don't we try a few together, and you can see which ones strike you?"

Duke Orsino reached past her and swept the remaining poetry books off the shelf and into his arms. At her look, he shrugged. "We might as well be thorough. Unless you had something else you needed to do today?"

"No." She hoped he didn't notice the slight squeak in her voice. She certainly hadn't planned to spend a large chunk of the day with Duke Orsino. Again. It did strange things to her heart, especially to see how determined he was to tackle these poetry books.

A resolve fueled by his love for Olivia. Viola had to keep telling herself that.

Carrying their armloads of books, they made their way to the front of the library, where they took a seat in one of the wide, cushioned alcoves beneath the tall windows, facing each other. The space was so wide that it didn't feel scandalous, and they could both sit comfortably without touching.

Yet they were still facing each other in a way that was cozy. Just the kind of cozy moments Viola had always dreamed about, when she thought about courting.

She piled her books on the cushions, and he did the same, spreading out the books in neat rows. "Where should we start?"

"How about this one?" Viola cracked the book open, flipping through it until she found a poem with which she was familiar. She read the first few stanzas out loud, then paused and peeked at him over the top of the book. His frown said it all, but she asked anyway, "What did you think?"

"Is all poetry this…incomprehensible?"

"Most of it is, especially many of the recent offerings coming out of the Court of Revels at the moment." Viola leaned forward and spread the book between them. "Perhaps discussing the poem together would make it more clear?"

He grimaced but nodded.

Viola pointed to each of the lines, pointing out what she thought it meant while giving him room to come to his own conclusions. It took a few stanzas, but the light grew in his eyes, and he steadily began talking more, contributing to the conversation.

With their heads bent together, the cozy alcove, his baritone filling the space between them, it was all Viola could do to keep her heart and imagination from running away with her.

This was just a part of her job as librarian. That was all. This meant nothing to him, so it needed to mean nothing to her.

As they moved on to new poems in another book, Belch slithered out of the bookshelves and up the side of the cushioned alcove—how he did it, Viola didn't know. She'd never quite been able to determine how the legless, wingless creatures managed to climb to all sorts of odd places in the Great Library, and it seemed the same held true here.

Belch wormed onto Viola's lap, giving a burp as he settled into place, and she scratched behind his ruff. It was a strange feeling, scratching the hard, yet pliable dry scales, but one that she was used to after so many years in the Great Library. The bookwyrm gave off a growling, purring sort of sound, vibrating his whole body beneath her hand.

Duke Orsino didn't do more than glance at the bookwyrm before going back to the book. Not in a dismissive way. More that he was so used to the creature that he didn't need to give it more than a glance.

Instead, the duke's frown deepened as he glared down at the current book open between them. "This one is even worse than the last one."

Viola skimmed the page, then stopped scratching Belch to shut the book. "You're right. That one is definitely worse than the last."

She tugged a different book off the stack and opened it. "Let's try this one."

Duke Orsino turned it slightly more toward him, probably to better read the scrolling font that sprawled amid illustrations of animals. "This is a book of ditties and limericks for children."

"Exactly. I realized I'm starting at the wrong place. We need to start at the beginning." Viola grinned and flipped to the first page.

Belch gave her a slightly affronted look—probably not amused that she had stopped scratching him—and slithered from her lap.

"I highly doubt studying ditties and limericks will help with Lady Olivia." Duke Orsino glanced from her to the book, his frown deeply etched from the grooves around his mouth all the way to the puckers across his forehead.

"Perhaps not, but you clearly need to have a bit of fun with poetry before we can move on to the more difficult stuff." Viola gave a shrug, trying to keep her grin under wraps. "Ditties and limericks are all the rage in many of the royal courts across the Fae Realm. Even if such knowledge doesn't help with Lady Olivia, it won't hurt the next time you attend an event at another court."

Duke Orsino raised his eyebrows and glowered at her. "Do you truly think I'm about to start spouting limericks at a court event?"

"No, likely not." Viola grinned right back, not flinching under his glower now that she knew it was more for show than true anger.

Somehow, she couldn't see Duke Orsino going about reciting inane rhymes the way her sister Brigid did when she wanted to convince others that she was particularly brainless. All a part of her cover as the Wild Fae Primrose.

A pang shot through Viola. Where was her sister at the moment? Caught up in whatever trouble had struck the Court of Knowledge and shut down the Anywhere Doors?

Luckily Brigid had been in the Court of Knowledge to see Sebastian and Viola off. Any other time, she and Munch might have found themselves stranded in a far-flung court much as Viola was now. Or, as Sebastian likely was, lost between the realms.

That pang turned into something more like pain. Was Sebastian all right? Was he safe? Or would he be lost forever between the realms, never to be seen again?

"Librarian Viola?" Duke Orsino's glower had dropped into something softer as his eyes searched her face.

"I'm fine." She couldn't tell him that she had been worrying over the brother he didn't know was missing. She forced the smile back onto her face. "Your turn. Read the first limerick out loud."

During her distraction, Belch had crossed the cushion between her and Duke Orsino and was now sniffing the duke's trousers at his knee as if trying to decide if the duke was someone worth cuddling with or not.

The duke began to read the first limerick in a monotone that was totally at odds with the subject matter, a rhyme about a giant talking snail taking a bath, a particularly ludicrous limerick since giant talking snails had a slime that was all but impossible to wash away.

Almost absently, Duke Orsinso reached out and ran his hand over the bookwyrm's head and down its back. Belch purred, then slithered onto the duke's lap, curling up as if planning to stay a while, mouth open slightly in the book-wyrm version of a pleased grin.

Duke Orsino finished reading the poem, but he continued to pet the bookwyrm, unbothered by finding the creature in his lap. "This limerick is the most ridiculous yet."

Viola didn't want to admit how appealing she found the sight of him with the bookwyrm. Even some of the librarians found the bookwyrms mildly creepy. She forced herself to smile and focus on the poem. "Yes, it is. I've always liked the slightly ridiculous ones."

Duke Orsino lifted his gaze from the book to regard her. "You truly love poetry, don't you?"

"Yes." Viola fidgeted with the hem of her librarian coat, not sure how much she should admit to him. "It isn't just the poetry. Plays. Fiction. Yes, even your stuffy reference books. I love all of them."

"You are a librarian." The lines around his mouth changed just enough to hint at a smile rather than a frown.

"It isn't just that." She dropped her gaze, trying to put her thoughts into words. Should she tell him this? "Seven years ago when I arrived in the Fae Realm, I was illiterate. I couldn't read my own name, much less even the simplest of books. But then my brother-in-law Basil taught all of us to read, and it was like the world opened up to me. I had the entire Great Library at my fingertips, and I couldn't read through the books fast enough."

"That's why you love them so much." Duke Orsino's voice dropped low, curling around her with the same comfort as a purring bookwyrm. "You never take the ability to read for granted. Every book that you can read—all the knowledge now available to you—is precious."

"Exactly." She shouldn't let the fact that Duke Orsino understood so completely go to her heart. He wouldn't look twice at her. He needed to marry Lady Olivia to fulfill the bargain. And the way he spoke about Olivia showed that he cared for her, beyond just the bargain.

What should Viola do? A part of her wanted to tell Lady Olivia that Duke Orsino wasn't like what she thought and she should stop avoiding him and simply talk.

But on the other hand, Viola didn't want to do anything that would end up breaking her brother's heart.

Assuming her brother was even still alive. What if he had died between the realms while Viola was sitting here, enjoying her time with the duke?

No, Sebastian couldn't be dead. They had survived the drought. Survived the move to the Fae Realm. Survived numerous monster attacks and fae machinations. Even survived a raid into the Realm of Monsters to rescue Munch and Brigid.

Surely he could survive this too.

Chapter Ten

Sebastian gasped as he dragged himself forward. Blood trickled from his nose while a metallic taste filled his mouth.

If he didn't get out soon, he wouldn't make it. Here, he didn't have to eat. He didn't have to drink. There was no time. He merely existed.

But with every moment, that existence was shredded away, leaving less and less of him. If he didn't escape soon, he might be completely torn apart, gone beyond hope of recovering himself.

Another red wild fae primrose. Another few inches forward. Another gasp for breath.

Then something hard and dark brown appeared in front of him. A horse hoof. Attached to a brown, horse leg. A brown, horse nose snuffled at his hair.

Or, to be more accurate, a shaggy brown pony with a white heart-shaped splotch on his nose and deep, liquid brown eyes.

Buddy nipped at Sebastian's hair. "This is quite the

predicament you've gotten yourself in. This is what comes of you leaving on adventures without my wisdom to guide you."

"Buddy," Sebastian croaked out through cracked lips. At least, he thought he did. He couldn't be entirely sure. It took all his strength to limply lift his hand and rest it on the pony's hoof.

As soon as he did, his head felt a hint more clear, his breaths a touch easier.

A figure in vivid red knelt next to him, and he had to blink several times to make out his sister Brigid. She rested a hand on his shoulder. "I'm glad I found you. Where's Viola?"

"Not here." Sebastian licked his lips. Parched, and yet not thirsty. Just shriveled and torn. "I think…I think she made it. Through the Door."

Brigid gave a sharp nod, then glanced over her shoulder. "Can you get him on Buddy?"

There must have been some kind of response because Sebastian's brother-in-law Munch appeared at Brigid's side, all browns and greens against Brigid's red, his bow and arrows on his back. Munch reached under one of Sebastian's arms and hauled him up. "Let's get you to your feet."

The motion sent Sebastian's head spinning, and he must have blacked out for a moment. The next thing he knew, he was flopped across Buddy's back like a sack of potatoes, his face dangling near Buddy's belly. He was a bit too big for the pony, but Buddy was sturdy and didn't give more than a grunt and a grumble at Sebastian's weight.

If he'd had more strength, he would have tried to scramble upright. But it was all he could do to keep his eyes open, and he caught only glimpses of their journey through the shivering space between the realms. Perhaps he was blinking. Or maybe he was passing in and out of consciousness. He couldn't tell.

At last, Brigid glanced at Munch, saying something too low for Sebastian to hear. Munch took his bow from his back and nocked an arrow. Brigid placed one hand on Buddy's neck, gripped Munch's sleeve with the other, then all of them stepped forward.

Something shivered over Sebastian, dragging at him one last time, before he popped out on the other side.

His head cleared. The weight on his lungs vanished. While his exhaustion remained, he could finally draw in a deep breath for the first time in far too long.

Sebastian lifted his head, propping his elbows against Buddy's side. He wasn't sure he was strong enough to stand just yet, but hanging with his head upside down wasn't going to help him recover.

Around him, the familiar trees of the Tanglewood formed a near solid wall to one side of the faerie circle while a meadow with a road leading to the village and the Great Library beyond ran along the other.

Despite being safe within their own court, Munch didn't put away his arrow or unstring his bow. If anything, he grew even more tense and wary, leading the way from the circle with careful movements and eyes darting about.

"What's going on? What happened?" Sebastian steadied himself as Buddy set off again, jolting him with every step.

"The Court of Revels attacked the Court of Knowledge." Brigid sounded as grim as he'd ever heard her.

Sebastian stilled, then slid from Buddy's back. He had to

brace himself against the pony's neck to stay upright, but his knees held. "They what?"

"They attacked. I'm not sure what King Oberon and Queen Titania are thinking." Brigid shook her head, her jaw tight in that look that boded ill for whoever she set out to ruin with her plotting.

"They aren't thinking, that's what." Buddy gave a loud, derisive snort. "The Deplorable Duo don't have enough brains between them to think up an attack like this. It's clearly the work of Claudius and his ilk from the Realm of Monsters."

If Sebastian's knees hadn't already been wobbly from his time between the realms, then they certainly would have been wobbly now.

"Yes, they seem to have the backing of Claudius and his wayward fae from the Realm of Monsters, but so far King Theseus and Queen Hippolyta have been holding their own." Brigid's eyes flashed. "I'm not sure what the Court of Knowledge would have done if we weren't aligned with the Court of Swordmaidens."

"A little help from forester iron hasn't hurt anything." Munch lifted his arrow, as if to demonstrate exactly what he meant.

"No, it hasn't." Brigid smiled one of those sappy smiles up at Munch. "You've been very helpful in turning the tide in more than a few attacks." She glanced over her shoulder at Sebastian. "It isn't even just the fae attacks. Rifts have been popping up all over, and monsters have been running rampant. It's all we can do to kill the monsters before they cause any real harm. If this keeps up, we might need to ask if one of Munch's siblings is willing to relocate to a war zone for a while to help deal with the monster problem."

Munch stiffened, spun on his heel, then drew back his bowstring in such a swift move that Sebastian hadn't even spotted the monster before Munch already had an arrow on its way.

The unusually sized rodent flopped onto its side, transfixed by the arrow.

"We'd better pick up our pace." Munch nocked another arrow to his bowstring. "Those rodents tend to run in swarms."

Sebastian tried to move faster, but his legs were aching, shaking, and nearly useless with his exhaustion. He gripped Buddy and stumbled along, half dragged by the pony.

"As you can guess, it has been a bit harried here the past few days." Brigid pointed, almost languidly.

Munch spun and shot twice, taking down two more of the rodent creatures.

"Harried is putting it mildly." Buddy made a snapping noise with his large, blunt teeth.

"We took a moment to plunge between the realms as soon as we could, but I'm sorry about the delay." Brigid glanced over Buddy's shoulder at Sebastian, her blue eyes crinkling with her true concern, even if her tone remained light. "I saw you were following the primrose path as best you could. Well done."

"I didn't do as well as you would have." Sebastian shook his head, then regretted it as soon as his head spun again.

"You haven't had the training I have. You found the primroses. You followed them. That's more than many would have known to do." Brigid's voice dropped under the weight of her true emotions. "You stayed alive. That's the important thing."

"Yes." He'd survived. Sebastian drew in a deep breath, taking a moment to savor that.

Munch loosed another arrow. A harpy screeched, gurgled, then plummeted from the sky.

Brigid held Sebastian's gaze again. "Are you sure Viola wasn't between the realms with you? I didn't get a sense of her there, and she wasn't anywhere near you, but…"

But if she was there, they couldn't leave her.

"I don't think she was." Even as he said it, a niggling filled his stomach. What if he was wrong? He'd thought Viola had gotten through the Door when he'd pushed her. But what if he'd been wrong? What if Viola had been there, just out of his reach, lost in the void with him? "I pushed her, and I think she made it to the other side. Hasn't she come back through the Anywhere Door to see what happened?"

Brigid and Munch shared a glance. Even Buddy remained silent, ducking his head as if he didn't want to be pressed for an answer.

"That's just it." Brigid halted, turning to face Sebastian squarely. "The Anywhere Doors have been shut down. It's a protective measure of the Court, buried deep in its magic, so it triggered as soon as the Court was attacked. King Theseus had no control over when the Doors went down or which ones. The only Door currently operating outside of our court is the one to the Court of Swordmaidens since they are our close allies."

Sebastian staggered to a halt facing her, digging his fingers into Buddy's mane. "Truly?"

This whole time he'd assumed that at least Viola was safe and in contact with the family. But she was just as cut off as he had been, all alone on the island.

He was supposed to have been there to introduce her to Olivia, Duke Orsino, the outpost, everything. Instead, she had been dumped into everything with no knowledge and no way to check in with the family.

"At least the Anywhere Doors inside our court are working." Buddy shook his head, whipping his mane against Sebastian's hand. "I don't know how I would deal with the stress if I couldn't get to my favorite clover patch."

Brigid patted Buddy's mane, then started walking again. "King Theseus has temporarily opened the Doors to each of the outpost libraries to let the librarians know what is happening and make sure all the outposts are fortified. But since the outpost on the Island of Melyria hasn't been officially established yet, it doesn't count to the magic of the court. The Anywhere Door won't open."

There was no way to get to Viola, and likely no way to even contact her until whatever war they were fighting with the Court of Revels was over. Whenever that would be.

But they couldn't just leave Viola there, all alone, not knowing what was happening.

She should be safe. Duke Orsino was honorable, especially for a fae. Lady Olivia would look after Viola, once she realized who she was and that she was alone.

Sebastian probably should stay here. Put his years of training with a sword to good use defending his court.

But he couldn't leave his sister there all alone, even though she should be perfectly fine. He wouldn't feel settled until he could check.

"I need to go after her." Sebastian tried to straighten so that he wasn't leaning on Buddy so much. "I know the rest of you need to stay here and defend the court, but I can't leave Viola there all alone."

"Admirable. Herd mentality and all that." Buddy nipped at Sebastian's shirt sleeve. "I'd go, but someone needs to stay and look after the children."

"And you do a great job of it." Brigid patted Buddy's neck, then met Sebastian's gaze again. "Rescuing anyone trapped between the realms was our first priority. But now that we know Viola made it to the island, someone definitely needs to get there right away. According to King Theseus, that sapling could put the entire Court at risk if something were to happen to it."

Sebastian's chest tightened again, as if he were still between the realms, struggling on his belly. Did Viola know how much danger she was in? She wouldn't know what was going on, cut off on the island as she was. "Any thoughts on how I can get there quickly? Can King Theseus open the door to the Island of Melyria just long enough for me to go through?"

"No. This magic is too deeply embedded in the court for even King Theseus to fully control. Once the outpost library is established, then librarians will be able to go through. Until then, that Door is locked tight." Brigid's mouth tipped into something almost like a smile. "The fastest way to get there is to take a ship from the Court of Swordmaidens. But…"

"I'm a man and thus forbidden to step foot on that island." Sebastian sighed and leaned more heavily on Buddy. He was too tired and sore to think clearly right now. "Will Queen Hippolyta make an exception?"

"That magic is deeply embedded in her court. I'm not sure how much wiggle room she has." Brigid swept a glance over him. "You wouldn't happen to want to win a swordmaiden's hand, would you? That is one exception."

"No." The word came out even before he'd thought about it too much.

Too fast.

"Oh, really?" Brigid raised her eyebrows, smirking at him. "That seemed rather definite."

He wasn't ready to tell Brigid about Olivia. It was too risky, since Olivia was still trapped in the bargain to marry Duke Orsino. If Sebastian and Olivia stated their intentions too plainly, it could count as her breaking the bargain.

Better to err on the side of caution, at least for now.

Instead, Sebastian put all his energy into rolling his eyes. "What I meant is that trying to win a swordmaiden's hand would take too long. There is a prescribed method for that. Even if I purposefully lost and Queen Hippolyta banished me from the island via a convenient boat headed toward Melyria instead of booting me through the Anywhere Door, it would still cause a delay over simply crossing the island and getting into a boat straight away."

"True." Brigid lowered her voice as they entered the village, walking between stone houses that were boarded up and quiet. So different from the usual bustle that filled this place. "There will be some delay, regardless. You're in no shape to go rushing off. You'll do no one any good, least of all Viola, if you show up at the island half-dead. I'm taking you home to get some rest. While you're resting, I'll consult with Queen Hippolyta, and we will have a strategy in place by the time you're ready to leave."

He didn't like it, but it was the most sensible plan. It was too dangerous to travel the Fae Realm while he was so tired. He would find himself shipped off to the wilds of the Realm of Monsters before he could blink if he let down his guard.

By the time they reached the House, he was leaning

heavily on Buddy again and barely awake. He managed to stay awake through the hugs with his older sister Meg, his nieces, and his youngest sister Beatrice. Then he collapsed onto his bed and promptly fell asleep.

"Is this truly the only way to get to the boat?" Sebastian eyed Minnie, the large goblin fae woman with the curving horns and facial features of a cow.

They stood between the columns in the Hall of Anywhere Doors that stretched between the Great Library and King Theseus's palace. Normally, this hall was filled with a bustle of fae coming from all over the Fae Realm to visit the Great Library.

Now, the white marble hall stood empty and echoing. The Doors were shut fast by magic.

"You will never step foot on the Island of Swordmaidens, thus obeying the laws of the court." Brigid grinned and gestured from him to Minnie. "I thought it quite a brilliant solution."

"You would." Sebastian grimaced and held up the strip of cloth. "And the blindfold?"

"An extra precaution." Brigid shrugged and hefted his pack on her back. "If you want to get to Viola as quickly as possible, this is the only way to do it."

Sebastian sighed and tied the blindfold over his eyes. He would do a whole lot more than this to get to his sister. "Let's do this."

He'd already said farewell to the rest of the family. There was nothing to do but stand there and try not to get in the way as Minnie heaved him over her back. Her horns brushed his back, but she didn't accidentally gore him.

Then they were moving. Sebastian squeezed his eyes shut beneath the blindfold, not willing to risk even an accidental glimpse.

With the Court of Knowledge under attack, it would never do to bring down adverse magic on their heads.

A door opened, then the shiver of passing through an Anywhere Door prickled over Sebastian's skin. Thankfully, it was only the normal whirl, over in less than a heartbeat, rather than the tangled shredding he'd endured when stuck between the realms.

Then warm sun beamed onto the back of his neck while a breeze scented by hot sand and salty ocean toyed with his hair.

Minnie carried him over what felt like some kind of varied terrain. The sounds of the ocean grew louder, punctuated with the cries of gulls.

Then there was the creaking of a wooden dock beneath Minnie's feet, and the shouts of sailors on a ship.

More wood creaked. Minnie's shoulders tensed beneath him as they seemed to be going upward.

Then Minnie knelt and he was set back on his feet. Sebastian straightened and pulled the blindfold from his eyes.

He stood on the deck of a small, ocean-going vessel with raised sections of the deck fore and aft with a large, square sail flapping against the single mast. The fae on the ship varied from a three-foot tall sprite with orange skin to a faun with shaggy brown goat legs to goblins with their animalistic features. A few of the sailors had bronzed skin and black hair cut short so that their tapered ears were clearly visible.

But most surprising was the dark-skinned man with the rounded ears of a human. Was he here willingly? Or had he been snatched by the fae?

Hopefully it was the former. That would be the safer option for Sebastian. If it was the latter, then Sebastian wouldn't dare sleep this entire boat ride to the Island of Melyria.

Then there was the flag flying from the masthead. Instead of the blue flag of the Court of Islands or the standard of one of the individual islands, this ship was flying the black flag with white, crossed bars that was the flag of the freebooters. At best, the freebooters were honest sailors with no affiliation to any island or court. At worst, they were pirates.

The human stepped forward and held out a hand in the human style of greeting. "Welcome to the *Snatched Revenge.* I'm Captain Antonio."

"You're the captain?" Sebastian shook the man's hand, though he couldn't keep the surprise from his tone.

"The Court of Knowledge isn't the only court where a human can find a place here in the Fae Realm. Or, not-a-court as the case might be." Captain Antonio smiled, then gestured at his ship. "You are fortunate that I happened to in port when I received word from Queen Hippolyta. My ship is safe for you."

Sebastian certainly hoped that Captain Antonio was telling the truth. He didn't have many options at this point. But a pirate ship didn't exactly seem the definition of safe.

Brigid halted next to Sebastian and held out his pack. "I wish I could go with you."

"You're needed back at the Court." Sebastian gave her a quick hug. "I can handle looking after Viola. She probably isn't even in any danger."

"I hope so. I hate to think of her facing something dangerous all alone." Brigid hesitated one more moment before she turned and marched down the gangplank after Minnie.

Sebastian picked up his pack and faced Captain Antonio, the crew, and the sea.

He was coming. Viola just needed to hang on for a few more days.

Chapter Eleven

Favian strolled the paths crisscrossing the island, his hands in his pockets.

He'd had enough of waiting politely for Olivia to answer one of his messages. He was going to talk with her in person and solve this once and for all.

As he passed by homes and other islanders, he waved and nodded or exchanged greetings as the case might be. But he didn't linger for longer conversations.

By the time he reached Lady Olivia's estate on the far side of the island, it was mid-morning, and the sun beamed down hot against his back and coat. Only the sea breezes kept him from sweating beneath his coat.

He halted before the door, raised his hand to knock, but paused. If he knocked, the maid would answer, and he'd likely be turned away as he had been so many times before.

It was the height of presumption and rudeness, but he stepped off the stoop and instead followed the path around the side of the house to the gardens.

The winding trails through the gardens remained as

familiar to him now as they had been when he had been growing up. A few of the trees were taller. The bushes thicker. The flowers fuller. But still the same paths he'd run as a child.

As he rounded a corner, he spotted Olivia strolling next to a fae man dressed all in black. The fae man was a good decade older than Olivia or Favian, and the lines on his face drew his mouth into a scowl that made Favian's own relaxing frowning face appear friendly.

Olivia's shoulders were stiff, her stance wary. The sight made Favian's own shoulders stiffen, his fists clenching at his sides.

In the bushes at the far side, one of Favian's guards, a faun wearing a green shirt to better blend with the foliage, kept a wary eye on Lord Chauvlyn.

Favian stalked toward Olivia and the fae male—Lord Chauvlyn, presumably.

Olivia's gaze remained fixed on the ground, so she didn't seem to see Favian right away. But Lord Chauvlyn halted, a curl of a sneer tugging at his lips. "Who do we have here?"

Olivia's head jerked up. "Favian…Duke Orsino…"

Favian halted, facing them. Why did she look so terrified at the sight of him? If she told him what he had done, he would correct the problem immediately. "Lady Olivia. Lord Chauvlyn, I presume."

"I see my reputation has preceded me." That sneer grew on the fae lord's face.

Favian chose to ignore that comment. Lord Chauvlyn might be a lord in his own court, and a lord trusted by his king. But Melyria was Favian's island. He was the duke here, and that meant he outranked Lord Chauvlyn. "I am not sure if you are aware, Lord Chauvlyn, but Lady Olivia is betrothed to marry me due a bargain between our fathers."

"Has it occurred to you, Duke Orsino, that perhaps Lady Olivia has no wish to marry you?" Lord Chauvlyn cocked an eyebrow along with that perturbing curl to his mouth.

Favian risked only a glance at Olivia, but her gaze was down again. She made no protest either way to Lord Chauvlyn's statement.

"Whether she wants to marry me or not is between her and me. You have no business sticking your nose into our affairs." Favian crossed his arms.

Lord Chauvlyn's eyes flashed at the word *nose*, and perhaps Favian shouldn't have used that phrase, given Lord Chauvlyn's rather large proboscis that was far more prominent than most fae's.

But then Lord Chauvlyn's expression smoothed back into that arrogant insouciance. "It is my business if I wish to offer Lady Olivia a way out of a bargain that she finds distasteful."

Favian couldn't help a flinch at that, his gaze shooting to Olivia again. Did she find the bargain their fathers had made distasteful? He hadn't thought so. They had been good friends, after all.

Yet what other reason could there be for her refusal to see him these past months and years?

The thought of his childhood friend despising him hurt more than it ought. Especially since he only had Lord Chauvlyn's assertion. He had yet to hear the truth from Olivia.

"Olivia?" Favian turned to her, his gaze searching her face, his tone soft. "Is that true?"

Olivia froze, her gaze still fixed on the ground. Then, she gripped her skirts, poised to run. "I need to go."

With that, she whirled and raced back to the house at a pace that was just barely ladylike.

"Ah, there, you see. She can't stand to be in your company." Lord Chauvlyn smirked, crossing his arms as he glanced between Olivia's fleeing form and Favian.

"Or perhaps it is you she's fleeing." Favian stepped closer and jabbed Lord Chauvlyn's chest with a finger. "Stay away from her."

"You might be the duke, but you have no authority to bar from me Lady Olivia's company if she wishes to allow it." Lord Chauvlyn didn't flinch beneath Favian's finger. "I am a guest here."

"You are not here by my hospitality." Favian jabbed Lord Chauvlyn with another finger. "Thus it would be a stretch to call on the laws of hospitality to protect you."

"Perhaps." Lord Chauvlyn's smirk never wavered. "But you will not risk your island to find out."

With that, Lord Chauvlyn spun on his heel and marched from the garden in the opposite direction from Olivia.

For a long moment, Favian just stood there. Lord Chauvlyn was indeed as slimy and distasteful as Sebastian had warned. He would need watching to ensure that he did nothing to either tamper with the bargain or otherwise jeopardize the island.

The bargain. Was that the reason Olivia had been avoiding him? But if she was struggling with the realities of the bargain their fathers had made, why didn't she just come to him? He was as stuck in the bargain as she was. If anyone could understand, it would be him.

It didn't make sense, and he wasn't sure what to do

about it. The look on Olivia's face when she caught sight of him made him hesitate to push her.

He would have to continue composing that poem he had started after spending the afternoon with Viola. He just had a few lines to add, then it would be ready.

Or, maybe it would be ready. Perhaps he should have Viola read it over first to make sure it wasn't completely rubbish.

After leaving Olivia's garden, Favian marched back across the island, turning over phrases and images to use for the final few lines.

For some reason, it was Viola who came to mind while he contemplated the poem, not Olivia. Perhaps it was only natural, since he had spent so much time discussing poetry with her.

Yet he was thinking of metaphors for golden hair and blue eyes rather than dark brown.

He shook himself. He was writing this poem for Olivia, not Viola. He had to keep that in mind. Whatever Lord Chauvlyn might say, the bargain wasn't going anywhere.

Favian couldn't let himself brush aside his integrity by letting himself fall for Viola when he was going to marry Olivia.

Merely forming a friendship with Viola wasn't wrong, was it? She was one of the librarians stationed on the island. Favian should form a good working relationship with her and her brother Sebastian.

That was the only reason he fully intended to make his way to the outpost library, as he had been doing nearly every afternoon for the past few days.

That, and he probably should make sure Lord Chauvlyn

hadn't bothered the librarians. The fae lord was, indeed, quite slimy.

VIOLA STOOD BEFORE THE BOOKSHELF, a paper on a board in one hand, a pen in the other. It took a great deal of time, but she cataloged each book one by one. Once the sapling was planted and the magic of the Great Library flowed into this outpost, the list itself would become magical, automatically noting when a book was loaned out, and who it was loaned to, and so forth. The list would also be added to the archives in the Great Library itself, where a list of all the books in the Great Library and all the outposts were kept.

Only a few more days until the full moon and the night she could plant the sapling. Only a few more days until this library wasn't so defenseless and she could finally breathe a bit easier.

At least the guards outside provided some reassurance. She wasn't as alone as she had been when she first arrived. So far, Lord Chauvlyn hadn't come anywhere near the outpost.

Which was suspicious, in and of itself. He seemed content to hassle Lady Olivia, but he hadn't so much as approached the outpost. What could he possibly be planning?

If only she was cunning, like her sister Brigid. Then she could figure out what Lord Chauvlyn's plan was instead of just sitting here, guarding the sapling and hoping she could head him off once he made his move.

Perhaps Lord Chauvlyn had made himself scarce since

Duke Orsino had been such a frequent visitor to the outpost library the past few days.

As if on cue, Duke Orsino's steady footsteps strolled behind her, halting a few feet away. "Good afternoon, Librarian Viola."

She nodded to him, smiling. "Good afternoon. What brings you back so soon?"

He rocked back and forth, then held out a piece of paper. "My attempt at a poem. It isn't very good, and it isn't finished yet."

Viola took the paper and steeled herself. No matter what, she wasn't going to laugh. She wasn't going to criticize. Just give constructive feedback where needed.

She quickly read the poem, schooling her features. It wasn't bad. Not necessarily great, but not bad either. Just a bit stilted and stiff. A bit like the duke himself. Not given to flights of fancy or long-winded spiels.

But it still warmed something inside her, knowing how much work he put into it. And a few of the phrases…

No, this poem was for Olivia. Not for her.

"This is a good, solid start for a poem." Viola handed the page back. "I can see where the work over the past few days has paid off."

"But do you think Olivia will appreciate it?" Duke Orsino glanced between her and the paper he held.

Viola hesitated. She didn't want to promise anything when she couldn't be sure how Olivia would take this poem.

If anything, Olivia wouldn't like it, since she loved Sebastian.

But Viola didn't want to hurt Duke Orsino by telling him that particular truth. "How could she not appreciate the time and effort you put into this?"

She snapped her mouth shut before she added, *I certainly do.*

Duke Orsino stared down at the poem, his mouth flattening, before he folded it and slid it into an inside pocket of his coat. "Perhaps."

There was something doubtful in his tone, his eyes more sad than they had been the last time she had seen him.

"Is something wrong?" Viola gripped her board and paper in both hands, hugging it to her.

Duke Orsino shook himself, then smoothed his expression. "No. At least, nothing worth mentioning."

It sounded very much like something was wrong, but it wasn't her place to pry. Nor did she really want to. She already had far too many secrets she was carrying around. Her secrets. Sebastian's secrets. Olivia's secrets. She didn't need Duke Orsino's secrets on top of it all.

Duke Orsino shrugged and seemed to slough off his melancholy. "What is your task for today?"

"I'm cataloging all the books. Once the outpost is officially established, this list will keep track of all the books in the library." Viola turned back to the shelf, trying to find her spot.

"Even more organization measures. I heartily approve." Duke Orsino stepped forward. "Is there any way I can assist?"

She nearly blurted out *yes* before she thought better of it. Spending even more time with the duke would only hurt her heart worse.

But she couldn't just turn him down either. He was the duke of the island, after all. "While I would appreciate the offer, don't you have paperwork of your own to take care of?"

Duke Orsino shrugged. "The thing with a small island like this is that it takes less paperwork to run than a full court. Cesario knows where to find me if I'm needed."

Well, there went that handy excuse. It wasn't like she was opposed to the duke's presence. He had a knack for efficient organization. The library wouldn't be in the state it was if not for him, especially since she was doing this on her own.

Not to mention he had seemed so melancholy a moment ago. She didn't have the heart to send him away when he'd sought her company for solace.

Her heart won out over her head.

She reached into her librarian coat and pulled out a piece of paper, pen, and a writing board and handed them to Duke Orsino. "In that case, why don't you start on that shelf and I'll work on this shelf. It will go faster with two."

Duke Orsino took the items, but his gaze flicked to her at that last sentence. "Isn't your brother helping you?"

Shoot. She shouldn't have implied that she was here alone.

"He was here earlier but..." What convenient lie would make sense? She was starting to run out of excuses for why Sebastian wasn't here when Duke Orsino was around. "He decided to check the Anywhere Door again, then he was going to spend some time at the harbor, looking for any new books and seeing if he could find news about the Court of Knowledge from the incoming ships."

She would have to make an appearance at the harbor, if she could slip away from Duke Orsino later this evening. Just to make sure Sebastian showed up where he was said to be.

"My servants haven't brought me any news from the harbor nor have I received replies to my inquiries yet." Duke

Orsino paced a few steps away, focusing on the upper shelf she had indicated.

She wasn't that short, but it was still nice that he was there to take care of the upper shelves so that she didn't have to spend so much time craning her neck. "Sebastian and I know that you would have told us if you heard anything. But you can understand our need to look into it ourselves as much as possible. Our family is in the Court of Knowledge. If there's trouble, we need to know."

"I'm sorry you haven't been able to contact them. I understand how worried you and Sebastian must be." Duke Orsino wrote down a book title, then glanced up at the shelf again.

More worried than he knew. Not only was her family back in the Court of Knowledge likely in danger, but Sebastian was missing and probably in even more danger than they were.

There was nothing Viola could do about it but fret and try to keep this outpost library running as it should.

Oh, and keep the sapling safe, figure out what Lord Chauvlyn was doing on the island, pretend to be both herself and Sebastian, and sneak around keeping up Sebastian's secret romance with Duke Orsino's bargained betrothed.

Not complicated at all.

"Yes, but your help these past days has been much appreciated." Viola forced a smile, not wishing to dwell on the dangers surrounding her family.

She and Duke Orsino fell into a rhythm. They worked their way along their respective shelves at about the same pace so that they curved around the library together.

At some point during the afternoon, Duke Orsino

ditched his coat as he had before, rolling up his sleeves to his elbows. While it wasn't stifling in the outpost library, it was warm. Especially since she didn't dare open the windows as she had before. Such a move would let in the pleasant breezes, but it would also make it easier for Lord Chauvlyn to sneak in past the guards.

As they finished with yet another shelf, Duke Orsino set aside his pen, paper, and writing board. "You've been working hard this past week. Why don't you take a few hours to see more of the island? You haven't had a chance to see the shore yet, which is a tragedy."

Hot and sweaty as she was, the thought of walking along the shore in the crisp sea breezes sounded absolutely lovely. Since she had been by herself, she hadn't wandered the island as freely as she might have, if Sebastian had been here to go with her or to guard the outpost while she was out. Once she learned Lord Chauvlyn was here, she hadn't dared stray far.

Besides, it would be best to get Duke Orsino out of the library before he truly began to question Sebastian's disappearance.

"Give me a moment, and I'll be ready to go." Viola hurried into the shelves until she reached the back corner.

She had left the sapling in its basket in a patch of sunlight while she and Duke Orsino had been working. But she didn't dare leave it there when she went out, especially with Lord Chauvlyn lurking about.

She gave a sharp whistle, and the four bookwyrms popped out of various nooks and crannies. She glanced between them. "Who would like to go with me to the beach this afternoon?"

Both Belch and Feste slithered into the basket. Feste

settled down, as if to sleep, while Belch's mouth hung open, his tongue lolling, as if he were a dog eager to go on an adventure.

Guess she was taking two bookwyrms along. She picked the basket up, propped it on her hip, then she faced the remaining two bookwyrms. "Keep an eye on the outpost while I'm gone."

Curio huffed a breath, wisps of smoke curling from his nostrils. Then he and Toby disappeared back among the shelves.

That done, Viola strode back the way she'd come and rejoined Duke Orsino. He didn't question the presence of the basket, sapling, and bookwyrms. He held both her librarian coat and his own coat draped over the arm that he held out to her.

She took it, strangely thrilled despite how odd it was to be escorted like she was some fae noble lady instead of a human librarian born on a dying farm.

They strolled from the outpost library, through the small garden, then onto the porch that surrounded the palace.

Duke Orsino paused to give a few murmured instructions to a servant—a willowy woman with aqua hair—before he escorted Viola along the length of the porch to a set of stairs set into the cliffs at the rear of the palace.

Viola caught her breath at the top, gripping the rail. They stood so high up, the breeze whipping from the sea to toss her hair and her skirts. Far below, the waves crashed against the boulders scattered across a sandy shore. At the base of the cliffs, a strip of sand gleamed invitingly.

"I've never walked along a beach before. Or touched the ocean." She hadn't meant to say it out loud.

Duke Orsino halted behind her, his hand only inches

from hers on the rail. "Really? I can't imagine never living by the sea."

"You've been spoiled." Viola shook her head, then forced herself to walk down the stone steps. Despite being stone, they were less slippery than she had expected, and the metal railing—some kind of faerie steel, no doubt—remained firm on one side while the cliffs soon rose at her other side.

After well over a hundred stairs—those were not going to be fun on the way up—she stepped from the last stone step onto the shifting sand.

Perhaps it was undignified, but sand like this just demanded that she take her shoes off. She quickly pulled off her shoes and buried her toes in the warm sand. Years ago, she'd gone everywhere barefoot. They had been too poor to afford shoes. But the hard, rocky ground of their farm had never felt this soft beneath her toes.

Duke Orsino strolled past her and draped their coats over a nearby rock. Then, inexplicably, he propped one foot on the rock and began unlacing his boot.

Rolling up his sleeves had been bad enough. But she could hardly comprehend the sight of the frowning duke hopping from one foot to the other as he took off his boots and stockings, leaving him standing in the sand barefoot with his trousers rolled up to his knees. The collar of his shirt was open, the fabric flapping in the breeze blowing from the water.

Then he glanced up, his deep brown eyes meeting her gaze. His mouth curved upward, changing the deep lines around his mouth into something warmer, brighter.

Viola struggled to drag in a breath past her pounding heart. She had been right. When Duke Orsino smiled, he was, indeed, more than a little handsome.

Giving herself a shake, she nestled the basket with the sapling into the sand in the shade of the boulder where the sun wouldn't dry it out too much. It would be safe as long as she and Duke Orsino didn't stray far. On this open beach, they would be able to see if anyone was trying to sneak up on them to steal the sapling.

Feste wormed her way from the basket onto the top of the rock, sprawling in the hot sun with a contented sigh.

Belch plopped onto the sand and dogged Viola's heels as she picked her way down the beach, the sand shifting beneath her feet with every step. Near the water, the sand transitioned from hot and shifting to more solid, cool, and damp.

The waves crashed into white foam, washing over the sand and Viola's feet in a cold dousing of water.

She couldn't help the squeal as she jumped back. "That's cold!"

"It's refreshing." Duke Orsino halted next to her, his toes burrowing into the sand as another wave washed over their feet, foaming white around their ankles.

This time she was prepared for the water, and she didn't jump back.

Belch sniffed at the water, then slithered in and out of the reaching edge of the waves, alternating between dousing himself in the water and coating himself in sand.

As her skin grew more used to the cold, Viola waded deeper, holding her skirts up to her knees, though the cresting waves still soaked the hem.

If she had been here with Sebastian, she would have splashed him. He would have splashed her in return, and by the time their water fight was over, they both would have been sprawled in the surf, soaked to the skin and laughing.

Even though Duke Orsino had rolled up his sleeves and his trousers, the sea breeze toying with the open collar of his white shirt, he was still too much a stuffy fae lord for her to dare splash him.

"It must have been pretty idyllic, growing up here." Viola dipped her fingers in the surf, letting the foam play through her fingers.

He shoved his hands into his pockets. "My parents used to take me to this beach when I was young. Olivia and her parents would come, and we'd spend hours swimming and building sandcastles."

"You and Lady Olivia sound like you are close." Viola wasn't sure why a stab of something almost like pain lanced her heart.

The emotion couldn't be for herself. Surely it was for Sebastian and Olivia. And for Duke Orsino, who seemed to care for Lady Olivia, even though she had fallen in love with someone else. He just didn't know it yet.

"We were." Duke Orsino sighed and shuffled a bit deeper into the water. "I'm not sure what happened that she won't even talk to me now."

Perhaps the pain was actually anger. How dare Lady Olivia—and by extension, Sebastian—hurt Duke Orsino like this? He was an honorable fae lord. Surely he would understand if they just explained the situation.

But they were keeping this secret, and Viola wasn't sure she dared be the one to tell it. Especially since she had enough secrets of her own to hide. Including the fact that Sebastian wasn't even here.

Should she tell Duke Orsino the truth? She'd been afraid that he would shut down the outpost library if the head librarian, Sebastian, wasn't even there to found it. But her fears had been groundless, based on a bad first impression. Duke Orsino would likely help her even more if he knew the truth.

But if she told Duke Orsino that Sebastian was missing, she would also have to tell Lady Olivia. And if she told that secret, then how many other secrets should she tell? Would exposing all those secrets now just make the whole situation worse?

Then there was Lord Chauvlyn. She couldn't risk him finding out that there was only a lone librarian guarding this outpost library instead of two of them. The more people she told, the more likely it was that Lord Chauvlyn would catch a whiff of the truth.

As painful as it was, she had to continue pretending to be both herself and Sebastian for the time being. She would only have to keep the secrets until the sapling was grown. Once the outpost library could defend itself—and thus her —she would tell Duke Orsino everything.

Duke Orsino turned to her, that hint of a smile banishing the frown again. "Have you ever built a sandcastle?"

"No." Viola turned from the water. "What do we do first?"

Duke Orsino knelt in the sand, heedless of his clothes, and began digging as he explained all the technical details of using the right sand and moisture content for sculpting the perfect sandcastle.

Viola knelt in the sand across from him, and she didn't try to hide her smile as she followed his lead. They soon had towers and moats and bridges sculpted out of sand. Belch slithered in and out of the sand tunnels, acting as if they'd built this castle just for him.

Sand coated Viola's hands, her knees, and her dress, but she didn't care. This afternoon was just the kind of new experience she had hoped for when she agreed to move to this outpost library.

She had just been expecting to share these experiences with her brother. Not a fae lord who was planning to marry someone else.

Was it wrong that she hadn't missed Sebastian most of the afternoon? It had been too easy to get caught up in the moment and laugh and smile without a thought for her missing brother or her endangered family.

She had never made memories by herself before. Spreading her wings without her family—without even Sebastian—at her side was a new feeling. Was it wrong that it was as exhilarating as it was poignant?

Duke Orsino sat back on his heels and brushed his hands together. Some of the sand rained onto their castle, but most still clung to his fingers, refusing to come off. "Supper is here."

Viola glanced from him to the stairs built into the cliff. Cesario and several other servants trekked down the stairs, carrying baskets.

Duke Orsino stood, then held out a hand to her. She took it, the sand on their fingers gritty and rough. They washed their hands in the surf while the servants set up a blanket, a small open-sided pavilion that let in the breezes but shaded them from the sun, and laid out the picnic.

Viola brushed sand from her skirt, but it did little good. Her hem all the way above her knees was damp and crusted with ocean salt and sand. Her arms were turning a hint red while the skin on her face felt tight and hot.

Yet she wouldn't have traded the afternoon for anything.

She retrieved the basket with the sapling, then took a seat on the light blue blanket, nestling the basket next to her.

Feste remained on the rock, still sunbathing. But Belch joined them on the picnic blanket, sniffing at the various dishes. Probably already planning which morsels he was going to steal.

She took in all the variety of colors of food spread out before them. All of the food in the Fae Realm tended toward vibrant hues of pinks and greens and blues never found in food in the Human Realm.

Her quick scan verified that all of the food was safe for her to eat. Since she was bound to the Court of Knowledge, most food was safe. Yet faerie fruit would make a fae drunk and cause even a human protected by a court to be vulnerable to fae persuasions.

But Duke Orsino was honorable. He hadn't had his servants sneak in anything harmful to her.

"This looks lovely. Thank you for asking your servants to set this up, Duke Orsino." Viola reached for a plate and began filling it with food.

"Favian," Duke Orsino burst out, almost as if he hadn't meant to say it. He met her gaze, something warm in his brown eyes. "Please, call me Favian."

Viola swallowed. Such informality would be dangerous for her heart. But she found herself nodding.

She and Duke Orsino—Favian—lapsed into light conversation while they ate. Belch snagged several pieces of the roasted meat, gulping them down with very little chewing. Even Feste joined them after several minutes, taking her own portion of the food.

"I'm going to be hosting a party on the night of the full

moon to celebrate the founding of the outpost library." Favian set aside his plate, brushing a few crumbs of pink bread from his trousers. "I don't know if you have…I know you weren't expecting to be cut off from your court when you came so if…" He swallowed, not looking at her. "If you need anything for the party, you can always ask my servants."

"Something, as in a dress?" Viola forced herself to smile. "Yes, I have a dress nice enough for a formal party."

"Oh, good. I didn't want you to be caught out. Or feel out of place." Favian rested his forearms on his knees. "You are the guest of honor. Well, you and your brother Sebastian."

If only the dress was her only problem with the planned party. No, the worst part would be having to pretend to be both herself and Sebastian. No doubt Favian would want to treat both of them as guests of honor, putting them—her—in the spotlight. Would the glamour stand up to such scrutiny?

"I look forward to it." Viola worked to keep her smile in place, not showing her nerves. "Thank you for going to such trouble to officially welcome me and my brother to your island."

"It was the least I could do." Favian pushed to his feet and held a hand out to her. "The sunset is lovely tonight. Would you like to stroll along the beach?"

She glanced at the bookwyrms. They were still noshing on leftovers. Favian's servants were standing by, ready to clean up the picnic. The sapling would be safe, and she wasn't going far.

Viola took his hand, letting him pull her to her feet with a strong confidence that had her heart fluttering. Before she could get too caught up in the moment, he let go of her hand. They set out at the edge where the hard packed, wet sand transitioned to fluffy dry. The setting sun spread orange rays along the horizon and onto the white caps of the waves.

As the next wave rolled in, something white and rolling along the sandy bottom caught her eye. She bent and picked up a shell, its fanned top a pure white and the inside a blushing pink, complete with a hint of glittering sparkles unlike anything she would likely have seen in shells in the Human Realm.

She wandered along the beach at the edge of the water, picking up more shells. Favian wandered next to her, answering her questions but remaining silent in between. His quietness was comfortable and unobtrusive, not pressuring her or making her think he was bored while she explored the beach.

At the far end of the beach where it narrowed as it reached a tumble of boulders, she picked up what felt like a stone, but it looked like an opaque piece of pink glass. "What's this?"

"Sea glass, created from a siren's tear." Favian frowned down at the sea glass she held.

He said it so somberly, as if there was something inherently sad about a siren's tear. "Is it only sad tears that create sea glass? Or can they be created if a siren laughs until she cries?"

Favian opened his mouth, hesitated, then shrugged. "I don't know. I suppose I will have to ask a siren to find out. Or maybe one of the books in the library will have the answer."

"If the outpost doesn't have the answer, the Great

Library would have it." Viola turned the sea glass over in her fingers, melancholy washing over her like the waves crashing over her feet.

How long would she be cut off from home? Her family? The Great Library? When she'd stepped through the Anywhere Door, she had expected to be able to pop back through for a visit whenever she desired. But it had been a week, and she had no idea how much longer she would be cut off from them.

Favian stepped a little closer, though he didn't touch her. "I am sure we will have an answer to our notes soon. Perhaps before then, if your King Theseus reopens the Anywhere Doors."

She swallowed and nodded, staring down at the sea glass in her hand for a long moment. When she finally brought herself to look up, Favian had eased even closer, his hands reaching for her, but not touching her, as if he was waiting for permission or unsure what move would be proper.

"Until then, you aren't alone, Viola." Favian's voice dropped further, his gaze holding hers, as he gently took her hand, wrapping his large fingers over hers, clasping the sea glass in her palm.

Somehow she found herself standing rather close to him, and he wasn't dropping her hand. Instead he gazed into her eyes, swaying closer as something charged passed between them.

She didn't have a whole lot of experience with this sort of thing but it almost seemed like...was he about to kiss her?

She caught her breath, her heart pounding harder. If he did, she wasn't going to push him away. Her toes were already curling in the sand, her fingers aching to dig into his thick, dark hair.

Then Favian froze, his eyes shuttering, that frown digging lines into his face once again. He gave a little cough, dropped her hand, and took a large step back from her. "My apologies, Librarian Viola. I believe we should continue our stroll."

Her heart thudded into her toes, but she forced herself to nod. She had to swallow several times before she could force words out of her tight throat. "Yes, we should. I really ought to get back to the outpost."

She shouldn't be this disappointed. Of course Favian wouldn't kiss her. He was too honorable to cross the line into anything romantic when he was in a bargain to marry Olivia.

As they set out along the beach once again, Viola slipped the siren tear into her magical pocket. She wouldn't be cut off from her family forever. Someday, probably soon, the Anywhere Doors would be functioning again. Sebastian would be found. She would no longer be alone.

Until then, she would have to carry on with all the secrets and danger as best she could.

Chapter Twelve

A few days after spending the afternoon with Favian, Viola was cataloging more of the books in the outpost library. She only had a few more shelves to go before she would be finished.

And just in time. In only three days, it would be the full moon and she could plant the sapling, bringing the semi-sentience of the Great Library to this outpost.

She had never thought she'd plant the sapling on her own. Founding this outpost library had been Sebastian's dream more than hers. She had been willing to go along, but he was the one who arranged for this outpost. He was the one who did all the work of negotiating between Favian and King Theseus. He should be here to see it come to fruition. It seemed so very wrong that he wasn't.

She would just have to carry on. It was all she could do at this point.

Two sets of footsteps approached, neither of them Favian's now familiar bootsteps.

Viola turned, then froze.

One of Favian's guards halted before her, gesturing to the person behind him. "There is someone here to speak with you."

Lady Olivia stood there, her dark curls in a loose chignon underneath the discreet, dark gray hood and cloak she wore.

Viola peered closely at the fae lady. She didn't see anything that would indicate a glamour. Would Lord Chauvlyn take on a glamour like Lady Olivia's face?

Or was Viola merely being suspicious because she was running around with such a glamour?

Swallowing, Viola nodded and waved to the guard, letting him know that Lady Olivia was allowed to stay. Not that Viola truly had the authority to ban the fae lady from the library.

The guard bowed, spun on his heel, and marched from the outpost, leaving Viola alone with Lady Olivia.

The fae lady peeked at Viola, her eyes large and innocent. "Are you Viola? Your brother Sebastian has told me a lot about you."

Oh, right. Viola wasn't supposed to have met Lady Olivia yet. She'd been avoiding the lady, in case meeting her as herself would make it easier for Lady Olivia to see beneath the glamour.

Viola dipped into a hint of a curtsy. "I'm Viola. Who are you?"

"I'm Lady Olivia. I'm…" Lady Olivia trailed off, pressing her mouth shut as emotions flashed through her dark brown eyes. Then she smiled again, the momentary lapse into emotion banished behind a pleasant mask. "I'd like to speak with Librarian Sebastian, if he's in."

It was broad daylight. No way was Viola going to risk the glamour without the cloak of darkness to hide her.

"I'm sorry, but my brother is out at the moment." Viola put as much sympathy into her voice as she could as she rested her hand on Lady Olivia's arm. "Is everything all right? Is there something I can do to help?"

Lady Olivia stayed Lady Olivia. So either she was the real Lady Olivia, or Lord Chauvlyn was wearing a particularly good glamour.

No, this had to be the real Lady Olivia. Viola didn't think Lord Chauvlyn would have been able to stuff down his sneering attitude long enough to pretend to be such an innocent, retiring lady.

Lady Olivia blinked, a hint of tears shimmering in her eyes. Then she shook her head. "No. I had hoped we would be able to tell you everything when…but I can't. Not yet. It's too dangerous."

Viola made a sympathetic noise in the back of her throat. She couldn't tell Lady Olivia that she already knew what was going on. "I heard you and Duke Orsino haven't been speaking to each other. It has something to do with the bargain your fathers made, doesn't it?"

Lady Olivia just blinked even more rapidly, turning away from Viola and hugging her cloak tighter around her. "Yes. But I can't talk about it."

"Perhaps not to me. But maybe you should just talk with Duke Orsino. He seems like an honorable lord, especially for the fae." It wasn't Viola's place to tell Favian what was going on. He should hear it from Lady Olivia.

"He is. That's what makes everything so much worse." Lady Olivia shook her head, a tear trickling down her cheek. She spun back to Viola, swiping at the tear. "When you see Sebastian, tell him…tell him I'd like to see him. Our usual time and place."

Viola scrunched her eyebrows, as if she was puzzled by how cryptic that was. "All right. I will. Just…be careful. I'm worried about Lord Chauvlyn being here."

"I am too." Lady Olivia took a few steps toward the exit before she halted and turned back, her hands clenched tight on her cloak. "I hope when this is all over that we will have a chance to get to know each other better."

Without giving Viola a chance to answer, Lady Olivia swept around the end of the shelves.

Viola slumped against the nearest bookshelf, bracing herself. What did Lady Olivia want? She had sounded desperate, but she hadn't wanted to open up to Viola as herself.

Would tonight be the night she saw beneath the glamour? Especially now that she had met Viola as both her real self and as fake Sebastian.

Viola would just have to be careful. That was nothing new at this point.

Viola, in her Sebastian glamour, strode across the island in the early darkness of night. She kept a wary eye out. The last thing she wanted to do was run smack into Lord Chauvlyn. He was likely prowling around somewhere. He was the kind to go skulking through the dark.

She carried the basket with the sapling with her. Perhaps it made the sapling more vulnerable, having it in the open like this. But she didn't dare leave it behind either.

Curio had come along as well, curling up in the basket

around the sapling. The little wyrm wouldn't offer much additional protection, but it was strangely reassuring to have one of them along. The bookwyrm would likely smell and sense danger long before Viola did.

Despite her worries, the walk across the island was uneventful, and soon Viola took up a position behind the arbor, hidden from the bench.

At midnight, a figure appeared, her skirts rustling softly. As she neared the arbor, she held her arms out, as if expecting Sebastian to step out and gather her into his arms.

It was what he likely would have done, if he were here. But Viola stayed where she was, hiding behind the arbor.

Olivia let her arms drop before she hugged herself, standing there forlornly before the arbor. When she spoke, her voice held a depth of pain. "Sebastian."

"I'm sorry I haven't been present as much as we expected. It has been too dangerous with Lord Chauvlyn here and the Anywhere Doors locked tight." Viola hoped her voice sounded sympathetic and longing. Like Sebastian would have, though Sebastian likely would have been holding her tenderly and whispering in her ear.

The basket in Viola's arms lightened, then she felt Curio slither down her trousers.

"Lord Chauvlyn is the problem." Lady Olivia rubbed her upper arms, giving a shiver. "He has become more insistent. He wants to end the bargain on the night of the full moon."

They couldn't let that happen. Who knew what kind of magic would be unleashed if the bargain was broken in such a way? Especially on a full moon when the magic was so high?

But what could Viola do? She couldn't be in two places

at once. She had to plant the sapling that night, otherwise it would die and the outpost library wouldn't be founded. The Court of Knowledge would forfeit the bargain King Theseus had made with Favian for an outpost. It wasn't quite a bargain, but nearly as good as one. Would failure to establish the library cause some kind of backlash on the island or her court?

Yet how could she leave Lady Olivia to fend for herself?

In all likelihood, Lord Chauvlyn would be too busy enacting his real scheme—attacking the outpost library, probably—to bother with Lady Olivia.

How could Viola be certain what his plan was? She wasn't like Brigid, who could think three steps ahead of Lord Chauvlyn.

Curio slithered up to Lady Olivia, giving that growling purr.

Lady Olivia knelt and scratched Curio behind his scruff. When the bookwyrm snuggled closer, Lady Olivia plopped on the ground, heedless of her dress and the dewy ground.

Curio climbed into her lap, settling there like a contented cat.

It was to Lady Olivia's credit that Curio liked her so much. Bookwyrms had good instincts about people.

Viola had to come up with some way to keep Lady Olivia safe. Sebastian loved her, and she clearly loved Sebastian. Whatever happened, Viola couldn't let Lord Chauvlyn hurt her.

The best case would be for Lady Olivia to be somewhere else that night.

Viola hated to make promises to Lady Olivia that she couldn't keep—something that was especially dangerous here in the Fae Realm. But she was human. Hopefully she could skirt around the magic.

Swallowing, Viola drew in a deep breath. "Run away with me that night. Meet me on the shore by the harbor."

"And the bargain?"

"True love breaks bindings. Surely it can break a bargain in such a way that it wouldn't jeopardize the island." Viola wasn't sure if that was true.

But it wouldn't matter. Because she wouldn't actually be running away with Lady Olivia that night. Poor Olivia would spend a fruitless night waiting by the shore, and she would likely believe that Sebastian had jilted her. Viola might be messing up her brother's love life irreparably.

But Lady Olivia would be safe. Once this was all over, Viola had to trust that Sebastian would be able to explain his way back into Olivia's good graces again. Viola might never be Olivia's favorite sister-in-law, but so be it. At least Olivia would be safe.

"All right." Olivia's stance relaxed fractionally, her voice brighter.

Curio gave one last purr before he uncurled and slithered off Olivia's lap. He returned to Viola, crawling up her trousers and flopping back into the basket.

"Try to pretend everything is normal until then. We can't let Lord Chauvlyn know we have a plan." Viola hoped it would be enough.

It wasn't much of a plan. Certainly nothing like the layers upon layers of plots Brigid would have devised.

But it would have to be enough. It was all Viola had.

"I will." Olivia stood, brushing off her skirts.

"I need to go. I can't leave Viola alone in the library for long." It was strange to speak of herself in the third person.

But for this moment, she was Sebastian as far as Lady Olivia was concerned. "You should go back inside. Who knows where Lord Chauvlyn might be lurking. Fav—Duke Orsino has him under watch, but I don't trust that the guard will be able to keep Lord Chauvlyn in sight."

"I understand." Lady Olivia reached a hand toward Viola again. But when she didn't take her hand, Lady Olivia's expression and hand fell. She turned back to the manor, disappearing among the hedges.

Viola waited until Lady Olivia was out of sight before she left the garden as well, hugging the basket with the sapling and bookwyrm to her.

Paths were even more quiet than they had been on her walk to Lady Olivia's mansion. While the village by the shore was always bustling, no matter the time of day or night, this rural part of the island had few fae out and about. If she hadn't known that Lord Chauvlyn was lurking around somewhere, she might have found it peaceful.

Instead, she jumped at the slightest sound. A rustle in the bushes. A branch stirred by the breeze. A bird erupting from the undergrowth.

Curio, too, peered over the edge of the basket, more alert and wary than he had been on their walk there.

Despite the nearly full moon overhead bathing the island in silver, the shadows appeared deeper, the night darker, than it had been earlier.

The palace, with the outpost library tucked in its shadow, loomed on the hill, highlighted by the silver splash of moonlight.

Almost home. Just a little bit farther, and she would be safe.

"Librarian Sebastian."

Viola stiffened and froze at the sound of Lord Chauvlyn's voice slithering from the darkness. She clutched the basket to her, thankful she still wore the Sebastian glamour. In the darkness, hopefully Lord Chauvlyn wouldn't be able to see through it. As much danger as she was in as Sebastian, Lord Chauvlyn would be more hesitant if he thought himself facing a man who had trained with swords for years rather than a lone woman who didn't have any fighting skills to speak of.

Inside the basket, Curio gave a little growl.

Turning slowly, she searched for the source of the voice. But she didn't spot him until he moved, a black spot against the gray shadows. There was no sign of the guard who was supposed to be watching the fae lord.

The moonlight skimmed across Lord Chauvlyn's smirk as he took another step closer to her. "Coming back from visiting Lady Olivia, I see. What would the duke think if he happened to learn of these illicit liaisons?"

Viola swallowed. What would happen if Favian found out the truth, not from Olivia or Sebastian, but from Lord Chauvlyn? It would be a blow to find out that two people close to him had kept such a secret.

Should she tell him? Would it be better or worse coming from her as herself? He would still be hurt that Olivia hadn't come to him in person, but Viola could soften the blow, at least. Lord Chauvlyn would not. He would make it sound as bad as possible.

What would Favian do once he found out? Would he call Sebastian out in a duel? Viola didn't have a hope of taking her brother's place in something like that. Nor did she want to fight Favian.

If Sebastian failed to appear, it would be all over the

island in a matter of minutes that Sebastian had gone into hiding. Or was a coward. Or wasn't really there at all.

Ugh. What was Viola to do? No matter what she did, she was likely going to ruin her brother's life, all in the name of trying to save it.

No time to come up with a plan now. Right now, she had to face down Lord Chauvlyn.

She drew in a deep breath and faced Lord Chauvlyn as squarely as she could, much as she could imagine Sebastian doing. "What of it?"

"You have a choice to make." Lord Chauvlyn crossed his arms, eyeing Viola. "On the night of the full moon, who will you leave unguarded? Lady Olivia? Or your sister and the sapling? You won't be able to protect both."

"Duke Orsino has Viola and the outpost library well-guarded." Viola tried to put a self-assured tone to her voice. It was becoming easier to remember to speak about herself in the third person when she was wearing Sebastian's face.

"I suppose he thinks he does." Lord Chauvlyn gave a casual shrug. "But the duke has lived on a peaceful, idyllic island for far too long. He has no idea how to deal with a real threat."

Probably all too true. Lord Chauvlyn was canny, and he'd been associating with dangerous people. Duke Orsino likely wasn't much of a deterrent, even if it felt disloyal to think that Favian wasn't up to the task.

"But you are correct. Duke Orsino's guards are at least something. Poor Lady Olivia has far less protection." Lord Chauvlyn sauntered out of the shadows. "I know who I would choose to protect, if I were you."

With that, Lord Chauvlyn strolled past her, heading down the darkened lane in the opposite direction.

For long moments, Viola just stood there, hugging the basket to her chest in a way that probably looked very strange for Sebastian. Curio gave another low growl before he swiveled his head to peer up at Viola as if asking if he had done a good job.

Viola peeled one of her fingers off the basket so that she could pat the bookwyrm's head. "Good job. I don't like him either."

Hopefully sending Olivia off to the shore would be enough to keep her away from Lord Chauvlyn. Right now, the sapling had to be Viola's priority.

Chapter Thirteen

Viola smoothed the skirt of a peach dress, its skirt layers of ruffles with straps instead of sleeves, leaving her shoulders bare. She checked that the basket remained securely strapped in place at her side. It would make dancing awkward, but it was safer than leaving the sapling behind or strapping it to her back where the sapling could be snatched without her seeing it.

Toby curled around the sapling, settling in for a long night. She gave the bookwyrm a pat. Perhaps she would slip him some of the meat from the food tables. Assuming there was some kind of meat served and not just frothy desserts.

Tonight would be interesting. Would someone notice that she and Sebastian were never in the same room together? What if she was seen putting on or taking off the glamour? Worse, what if someone noticed that she and Sebastian seemed to keep passing the basket back and forth between them?

How was she going to manage to be Sebastian when anyone would see beneath the glamour if they touched her?

It would have been easier if she just refused the invitation. But she hadn't wanted to do that to Favian. Not when he was going through so much trouble to host this party.

She could have said that Sebastian had remained behind to guard the outpost. But that wouldn't make much sense since she wouldn't want to leave the sapling behind.

All so confusing. But after tonight, the secrets would be over. Once she planted the tree and it grew to full size, then she would tell Favian the truth. The tree would have enough of its own magic to protect itself. There would be no risk from Lord Chauvlyn. If Favian grew so angry that he tossed Viola from the island, then…

Then she'd be heartbroken.

Surely Favian wouldn't do that. He would understand the danger she had been in. Why she had lied. Hopefully.

With one last glance around her bedchamber, she stepped into the outpost library and navigated between the shelves. She took a moment to lay her librarian coat on the stones next to the cleared patch in the center of the library. It wouldn't match her peach dress, and the coat would be safe enough here until she returned.

A hint of the sunset glimmered through the skylight above. Soon the moon would rise. Viola would need to be back here just before the moon was high overhead, beaming down into the patch of dirt where she would plant the sapling.

As she turned the last corner of the winding bookcases, she halted, her heart giving a lurch at the sight of Favian standing there, hands clasped behind his back.

He wore dark gray trousers and a deep green jacket that mirrored the look of the green librarian coat she'd left behind, though with longer, more formal tails. His black hair lay smoothed over his head, with a hint of wave keeping the style from being too severe.

As she stepped out of the shadows by the shelves, he strode forward and held out his arm. "Would you allow me the honor of escorting you, Librarian Viola?"

She couldn't help but smile as she took his arm. "Thank you. I would like that."

Favian glanced over his shoulder at the bookshelves. "Is your brother coming?"

"He wants to do one last check to make sure everything is ready for tonight, then he will head over." Viola kept her smile in place, even as she internally winced. When had she become such a proficient liar?

Brigid was the one who could breezily lie like it was nothing. Viola hadn't been like that.

Until now.

After tonight, it would all be over. She just had to focus on that. Only a few short hours.

Together, she and Favian swept along the garden path between the outpost and the palace. Guards fell into step behind them, but Viola only vaguely registered their presence.

Her world had narrowed to the feel of Favian's coat beneath her fingers, the way their strides matched as the gravel crunched beneath their shoes, the tender look in his eyes when he glanced down at her.

It would be all too easy to get caught up in this moment. To think that Favian might be willing to find a way out of the bargain to marry Viola instead of Olivia.

But that was foolish. Perhaps Favian wouldn't have much of a choice in the matter, since Sebastian and Olivia seemed to be intent on wiggling out of the bargain regardless of what Favian wanted. But that didn't mean Favian would be happy to find himself free to court Viola.

After her brother stole away Olivia—assuming her brother made it out of the between safe and sound—and Viola revealed her lies, Favian likely wouldn't want to have anything to do with their family ever again.

As they neared the palace, the lilting sound of music drifted on the sea breezes. Light spilled onto the porch, creating shadows by each of the pillars.

The shadows didn't frighten her with Favian at her side. If Lord Chauvlyn was lurking, he wasn't going to attack her while she was on the arm of the island's duke.

The music wrapped around them, drawing them in, as they strolled into the palace. Only a few short stretches of hall brought them to the grand ballroom. One side of the room overlooked the cliffs and the ocean. Double doors filled with glass panes stood open, letting fae come and go onto the porch while the sea breeze teased the curtains on either side. A few dragonflies, puffing shimmering puffs of fire, flitted between the chandeliers hanging from the ceiling.

As they entered, several of the nearby fae halted, then bowed to Favian. He nodded in return, and Viola forced herself to smile and give a bobbed curtsy of her own.

Favian turned to her, his arm sliding under hers until, somehow, Favian was holding her hand, his deep brown eyes peering deep into hers. "May I have this dance, Librarian Viola?"

She swallowed and nodded. She didn't even get a chance to take in the ballroom before he was sweeping her onto the smooth, marble floor. She wasn't even sure of the steps, yet somehow she managed to relax and let him guide her without too much stumbling. Favian guided her so smoothly that the sapling in its basket, secured to her sash, bobbed gently as if it, too, enjoyed the dance.

Her feet might not be falling, but her heart sure was. Falling hard.

What was she going to do? Favian needed to keep his bargain and marry Olivia for the sake of his island. Viola had no business falling for him.

But she couldn't force herself to pull away when he was sweeping her around the dance floor, a real smile breaking through to replace the frown lines. That smile was filled with memories of making sandcastles, strolling along the beach, and long days working together to set the outpost library to rights.

Just for tonight, she was going to let herself fall. Hopefully the pieces wouldn't be too shattered when she had to pick them up tomorrow.

Sebastian clung to the rail, trying to hold on to his stomach. As he had found out during the last few days at sea, he was not cut out for the life of a sailor. He needed firm ground beneath his feet, not this pitching deck.

"We're almost there." Captain Antonio halted next to him, then pointed. "That smudge is the island."

Sebastian raised his head and peered into the growing darkness. A darker smear against the gray of sky and ocean broke the horizon. "Oh, good."

He wasn't sure how much more of this rolling he could take.

"Normally we would wait to dock until the morning, but

you mentioned this is somewhat time sensitive." Antonio gestured to the island.

"Yes. I need to be on the island before the full moon is at its zenith." Sebastian tried to straighten against the rail. He needed to gather his strength. He didn't know what kind of trouble he'd find when he arrived.

"It will be a tricky landing, but thankfully the harbor at Melyria is one of the largest and easiest to navigate in the Court of Islands." Captain Antonio tipped his hat to Sebastian, then turned to face the ship, barking orders to his men.

Sebastian gripped the rail, his gaze fixed on the smudge. Only a few more minutes, then he would reach Melyria.

The choppiness increased as the ship neared the harbor. In the fading light, any rocks lurking just below the surface were invisible, except for the white shimmer of the breakers against them.

Captain Antonio gripped the ship's wheel, shouting commands. The captain and crew seemed to be manipulating the sail in time with adjustments to the rudder to navigate the ship into the harbor. But even after nearly a week on this ship, the ship jargon still didn't make a whole lot of sense to Sebastian.

As the sun fully set and darkness deepened, a lighthouse on the point flared to life, sweeping a beam in a slow circle.

Sebastian gripped the rail, a part of him wishing he could just squeeze his eyes shut until this was all over and he was safely on land again. But another part of him didn't dare look away, as if by looking away he would cause the ship to crash.

The moon rose on the horizon, throwing silver beams across the ocean and marking the passing time. The ship was picking its way into the harbor with aching slowness. Sebastian didn't want to prod Captain Antonio to hurry, but that moon was going to be high in the sky before they knew it.

Finally, the ship drifted into place beside an empty dock. Two of the sailors leapt from the ship with ropes in hand, looping them around the bollards with expert twists. The ship's momentum snugged the ropes tight, finally halting the ship.

Sebastian peeled his fingers from the rail. He didn't have time to wait for the crew to set up the gangplank. He waved to Captain Antonio, then took a running leap through the opening in the rail. He cleared the churning ocean and landed on the dock, nearly falling to his knees.

Two fae were coming his way along the dock, holding lanterns high. "Sir?"

Sebastian stumbled forward, waving at the ship as he brushed past the fae. "The captain's still on board."

He only caught a glimpse of the fae's wide, startled eyes before he broke into a jog, focused on the end of the dock and the shoreline.

A figure wrapped in a cloak and walking along the beach in the moonlight caught his gaze. He wasn't sure why at first. It wasn't like he could make out a face past the dark cloak and hood.

Perhaps it was the way the figure moved. Or something subconscious that he couldn't define. Yet something deep inside him knew the person on the shore was Olivia.

When he reached the end of the dock, he jogged along the cobbled street, then down the rock steps to the sandy beach. His boots slipped in the sand, muffling his steps as he neared the cloaked figure.

Perhaps she had the same sixth sense, for as he approached, she turned, the moonlight falling onto her features. "Sebastian. I was beginning to worry."

"I'm here now." He gathered Olivia into his arms, holding her close. "I'm finally here."

Olivia must have been so worried when he hadn't made it through the Anywhere Door. What must she and Viola have thought, cut off as they had been for the past twelve days?

Olivia snuggled into his embrace, her hood falling from her head. "I've missed your arms around me."

"I've missed holding you," he murmured into her hair.

"You had a funny way of showing that the past few days." Olivia's arms tightened around him. "You wouldn't so much as sit next to me a few days ago."

Sebastian stiffened. What was she talking about? He hadn't been on the island a few days ago. "I—"

Olivia pulled away from him, pressing a hand over his mouth. "But I understand. Things have been tense, with the Anywhere Doors not working and Lord Chauvlyn on the island."

Lord Chauvlyn was here? What was going on? Sebastian tried to wrap his mind around it.

"But now that you've come tonight, everything will be fine. We will marry, and no one will be able to stand between us." Olivia lowered her hand to clasp her fingers with his.

"Marry? What about the bargain?" Sebastian squeezed her hand. He wasn't sure why he was protesting.

Olivia blinked up at him, her eyelashes limned with moonlight. "You said you had a way around the bargain. That true love would override the bargain."

Sebastian had said he had a way around the bargain before he'd left to fetch Viola and the supplies to found the outpost library. But it hadn't been true love.

"When did I say that?" Sebastian gripped Olivia's hands, searching her face.

"Just three nights ago." Olivia's eyes focused on him, her eyebrows scrunched. "You said we needed to get married tonight. Lord Chauvlyn has been trying to court me. He's been making threats."

Sebastian hadn't been here three nights ago. But someone had been.

He let go of Olivia's fingers and paced, dragging a hand through his hair before he clenched his fists. If he hadn't been here three days ago, then who had Olivia been talking to?

It sounded a lot like a glamour. He might have suspected Lord Chauvlyn of such trickery, but surely if Lord Chauvlyn had gotten his hands on such a glamour, then Brigid would have warned all of them.

No, the only one Sebastian knew with a glamour like that would be Brigid. She had a whole handful of glamour necklaces.

Had she given one to Viola? Brigid had pulled Viola aside moments before they left, but he hadn't registered if Viola was wearing one of the necklaces as they stepped through the Anywhere Door.

Why would Viola pretend to be him? Especially to fool Olivia of all people?

Then again, he hadn't told anyone who Olivia was to him. He hadn't told Viola that much about the island at all, really, expecting to show her around in person. She would have stepped through that Anywhere Door utterly ignorant, with a sapling to protect, a library to found all on her own, and Lord Chauvlyn skulking, presumably up to no good.

Viola wouldn't have dared let Lord Chauvlyn realize she was here alone, without Sebastian. Wise of her, especially since she didn't even know that the Court of Revels had attacked the Court of Knowledge and they were officially at war. But she knew enough of Lord Chauvlyn to be wary.

Why would Viola encourage him and Olivia to get married tonight? She wouldn't have known that Sebastian was going to show up.

"Sebastian?" Olivia took a step back, wrapping her arms around herself, her expression falling. "I knew something was wrong. You've been distant, ever since you returned from the Court of Knowledge. You've decided we can't get married. That I have to keep the bargain."

"No, no, it isn't that." Sebastian reached for her again, drawing her close. He couldn't imagine letting her go, watching her marry the stuffy Duke Favian Orsino. The duke was nice enough, he supposed. But not the one for Olivia. The duke would stifle her.

He didn't know what Viola's plan had been, but perhaps he shouldn't question it. He had nearly died between the realms. He'd come so close to never seeing Olivia again. Never marrying her. Never living all the dreams they'd made during their clandestine meetings beneath her rose arbor. What if he hesitated and he lost his chance entirely? What if marrying her was the only way to keep her safe from Lord Chauvlyn or the unwanted marriage to Duke Orsino?

Tonight was a night for doing something reckless.

Sebastian checked the moon. They still had a few

minutes until the moon was high. Fae marriages didn't take long.

Sebastian swept Olivia off her feet, cradling her in his arms. "All right, then. Let's get married."

She squealed, then wrapped her arms around his neck. "Really?"

"Yes." He didn't know why Viola—and it must have been Viola—had told Olivia that she and Sebastian needed to get married tonight. But he trusted his sister. Perhaps she had found out something he didn't know about the bargain, and that was why she thought true love would work. "It's about time, don't you think?"

"Yes!" Olivia hugged him tighter.

"Then in that case, I'm officially snatching you from your court." Sebastian strode across the sand. It shifted beneath his feet, making it harder to carry Olivia.

To start a binding between them, this was the easiest way to do it. Hopefully just stepping onto Captain Antonio's ship—and thus off the island—would be enough to count as snatching Olivia from her court. Sebastian didn't have the time to get her all the way back to the Court of Knowledge.

Sebastian peered around Olivia to find the stairs, then he bounded up them. He strode along the cobbled road, then back up the dock, passing the two fae going back the other way.

They both looked at him askance, probably since he had a fae lady in his arms.

Olivia pulled the hood over her face again, ducking her head as they passed the fae.

The ship was a hive of activity. A gangplank thankfully stretched between the dock and the ship. He wouldn't have been able to make the leap a second time while carrying Olivia.

Sebastian halted at the end of the plank. "Permission to come aboard again, Captain?"

Captain Antonio stopped his conversation and turned to Sebastian. "That isn't your sister, is it? Because you sure aren't holding her like a sister."

Sebastian laughed and held Olivia tighter. "No, she's not my sister."

"Ah. Well, come aboard." Captain Antonio waved them on.

Sebastian would have to give him a longer explanation later. Right now, he needed to find a quiet corner and as much privacy as possible.

Captain Antonio appeared at Sebastian's elbow. "Ah, Lady Olivia. It is good to see you again."

Olivia stiffened, her tone turning cold. "Captain Antonio. You're banned from Melyria."

"I've come to plead my case." Captain Antonio's genial smile fell from his face. "It wasn't my ship that plowed into your father's that day. I came across the wreck shortly after it happened, but there were no survivors. The ship from Melyria that came across me as I was plucking the bodies from the sea claimed I was the ship who attacked them. That's why I was banned."

In Sebastian's arms, Olivia sniffed and swiped at her face. "I always thought it strange that you would attack his ship. But then…"

"Your father and the late duke were good men. I would never hurt them. But I can understand why Duke Orsino and the island wanted someone to blame." Captain Antonio gestured to the stern. "You can step into my cabin for a bit of privacy, if you'd like."

If Captain Antonio knew Olivia, then he knew about the bargain. But he didn't question Sebastian or ask for the full story. If he had been another pirate, he might have suggested the room with a leer.

But he was sincere. He was merely offering the privacy of the room, knowing Sebastian was too honorable to cross any lines.

Well, perhaps not so honorable. Was it honorable to snatch Olivia and break the bargain like this?

It was for Olivia's safety. She needed to be protected from Lord Chauvlyn, and Viola had clearly been doing that as best she could.

Sebastian carried Olivia to the captain's cabin at the stern of the ship. Olivia had to open the door for him, then he set her down inside and closed the door.

It was dark in the cabin with only the moonlight streaming through the tiny windows ringing the window bench in the stern.

When he turned back to Olivia, he smiled. "A pirate ship isn't quite where I planned to marry you. I wanted to whisk you through the Anywhere Door to the most romantic spot I could find in the Great Library."

Olivia held out her hands to him. "Pirate ship. Great Library. I don't care. I just want to marry you."

Holding his breath, he took her hands. Was snatching her to this pirate ship enough to start a binding?

He shouldn't have worried. The moment his fingers touched Olivia's, their hands glowed.

Olivia smiled, meeting his gaze as she drew something

out of her pocket. A blue ribbon. One that had once been wrapped around a bundle of flowers he'd given her.

They clasped hands with the ribbon between their palms, then wrapped the ribbon around their hands so that they were bound together, repeating the words *With this binding, I pledge myself to you* as they did so.

After hearing from his brother-in-law Munch about the trouble he and Brigid had actually tying the knot, Sebastian might have practiced tying knots one handed. He and Olivia had left plenty of ribbon, so they were able to tie the knot without too much fumbling.

As soon as the knot snugged tight, the ribbon glowed and, in a flash, disappeared, leaving a golden ring around each of their wrists.

Sebastian drew Olivia in close and kissed her. They were married. No bargain or lord or duke could keep them apart ever again.

Yet even as he kissed her, the deck heaved beneath his feet in a way it shouldn't while tied to the dock.

Sebastian drew back, though he still held Olivia. "What was that?"

"Hmm?" Olivia blinked hazily up at him for a moment before she shook herself, her gaze clearing as another tremor passed through the deck. "Is it something with the ship?"

"I don't think so." Sebastian tilted his head, trying to listen.

Someone pounded a fist against the door, causing both him and Olivia to jump. Captain Antonio's voice spoke from the other side. "Sebastian, Lady Olivia. You might want to see this."

Still holding Olivia's hand, Sebastian opened the door and hurried outside, Olivia at his heels.

As soon as they stepped onto the deck, he caught sight of most of the sailors at the rail, staring at something on the island.

Sebastian followed the direction of their gaze, and his stomach sank. The faint sounds of screams came from the palace on the hill. Silhouetted against the palace was a black, twisty tear in the realms. A creature slithered out of it, its multiple heads dark in the silver moonlight.

They'd made a huge mistake. True love hadn't been enough.

Olivia's fingers squeezed his as she halted at his side, her face pale in the moonlight. "We broke the bargain."

"Yes." Sebastian set off for the gangplank, glad when she matched his swift pace. "We need to find Viola."

He'd messed up. He'd let his desires get the better of him.

Now all he could do was get to Viola and help her defend the outpost library. Then he would figure out how to fix what he'd just done.

Chapter Fourteen

With a final glance around, Viola slipped away from the party, clutching the basket to her. As much as it would have been nice if Favian escorted her, she didn't want to take him away from the party. Also, if she was sneaky, perhaps she could evade Lord Chauvlyn. She hadn't seen him yet tonight but that likely meant he was doing what he did best—lurking all sneering and sinister in the shadows.

Once Viola was out of sight of the party, she gripped the pendant and squeezed her eyes shut. She not only envisioned herself as Sebastian, but she willed the glamour to cover the basket as well.

When she opened her eyes, she seemed to be wearing Sebastian's librarian coat and the basket no longer appeared to be at her side.

She could still feel it there when she reached down. If she looked closely enough, she saw beneath the glamour.

Straightening her shoulders, she strode purposefully through the halls, then stepped out into the nighttime garden. A breeze whispered between the flowers, and she shivered. The glamour might make her look like she was Sebastian wearing a coat, but underneath she was still in nothing but a gauzy peach dress with nothing but straps over her shoulders.

The moon arched high overhead, bathing the garden in silver. Before stepping out from the shadows of the porch, Viola scanned the gardens. Two fae guards paced in front of the door to the outpost library, but that was the only movement.

Gripping the basket to her side, she stepped from the porch and tried to keep her stride casual and confident. She was Sebastian. She had years of training with a sword. She had no fear of walking across a garden at night. Albeit a very bright, moonlit night.

The hair at the back of her neck prickled, but she strolled across the garden without incident. She gave a manly nod to the guards, then she pushed open the door and stepped into the outpost library.

The library was cast in eerie shades of black shadow and silver moonlight streaming through the tall windows and the skylight overhead. With the spiraling shelves, she couldn't see far into the library.

But it was quiet. Too quiet? Except for the bookwyrm in her basket, she didn't see any of the others.

Perhaps they were waiting in the center, ready for her to plant the sapling.

She hurried through the library until she reached the dirt patch. The moonlight cast a stark, silver circle through the skylight, nearly directly overhead.

Time to get digging.

She picked up her librarian coat from where she had left

it earlier. Her vision went weird again, as she shrugged into her librarian coat while also seeing Sebastian's librarian coat already on broad shoulders. The warmth of her coat settled around her shoulders over the peach dress, its weight familiar and comforting.

A shudder trembled through the ground beneath her feet. She froze, waiting. What was that? Was that the faint sound of screaming?

She couldn't investigate now. She had to get this tree planted. The moon crept ever closer to right overhead.

She reached into her magical pocket and drew out a shovel. It would have been easier to dig if she'd truly been wearing Sebastian's boots and trousers instead of her slippers and dress beneath her library coat. But she didn't want to take the time to change.

Not that it mattered. She only needed to dig up one shovelful to create a hole for such a small sapling.

She set the shovel aside, then knelt. Gently, she picked the sapling out of the basket, unwrapped the burlap from the root ball, and placed the sapling in the hole. She tucked the dirt back around it, patting it in nice and firm but not too firm. After brushing off her hands as best she could—she likely would have dirt under her fingernails for days—she reached into the magical pocket of her librarian coat and pulled out a jug. Pulling out the stopper, she poured the water—taken from one of the ponds inside the Great Library—onto the sapling.

She glanced at the skylight. The moon beamed down from overhead, perfectly centered in the skylight.

Back in the Court of Knowledge, she'd envisioned sharing this moment with Sebastian. She wasn't supposed to do this alone.

She had no choice. This outpost library had been Sebastian's dream. Whether he was alive or dead there between the realms, she would make sure this tree was planted and this outpost was established.

Only Toby was at her side. Where were the other bookwyrms? Shouldn't they all have been here?

No matter. Viola placed one hand on the tree and one on the back of the bookwyrm. She wasn't as sensitive to the magic of the Fae Realm as her sister Brigid, but she thought she could feel the gathering magic as the moonlight seemed to swirl around them. "As a librarian of the Great Library, I establish this outpost library."

Silver sparkles glinted in the moonlight as they spun in eddies around her and the tree, coalescing onto the leaves.

She held her breath, taking in the magic. Beneath her hand, the sapling slowly unfurled, sending out shoots and leaves and growing by several inches every second.

Even as she watched, another tremor shook the ground beneath her. Were the screams and shouts growing louder? What was going on?

She didn't dare leave the tree. It was still growing, still vulnerable right now.

"I thought you would remain with Olivia." The flat baritone voice of Lord Chauvlyn shivered from the darkness behind her.

She whirled, still crouching. Right. She was still wearing her glamour as Sebastian.

As surreptitiously as she could, she glanced around. The shovel lay just out of reach. If she lunged, she might be able to grab it.

Then what? Lord Chauvlyn was a fae lord. Stronger and faster than she was. As much as she wanted to whack him in the head with the shovel, she wouldn't get anywhere close to hitting him.

"You must have done something to break the bargain, as I knew you would if I threatened Olivia enough." Lord Chauvlyn stepped from the shadows by the nearest shelves, three bookwyrms hissing and growling at his feet. "Duke Orsino truly is dense. It only took me a few days here on the island to figure out what Duke Orsino has yet to see. But you aren't much smarter. Certainly not as smart as your sister."

"What do you mean?" Viola eased a little bit closer to the shovel. As long as she kept Lord Chauvlyn talking, he wasn't enacting the rest of his plan.

"Rifts to the Realm of Monsters are opening all over the island." Lord Chauvlyn sneered, taking another step closer.

Her hand was almost to the shovel. It was the only thing she could think to do.

What did he mean about rifts opening up? She hadn't seen Olivia all night. She couldn't have done anything to break the bargain.

Unless Olivia's intent to break the bargain that night was enough? A scary thought. The Fae Realm usually operated more on the letter of the law than the intent. That was how Brigid managed to skirt so many rules.

Lord Chauvlyn reached into his pocket and drew out a long, shining sword. "Sebastian, Librarian of the Great Library, I challenge you to a duel."

Not happening.

Viola shook her head, bracing herself to lunge for the shovel. "No. Not interested."

Lord Chauvlyn raised an eyebrow and brandished the sword in her general direction, though he didn't put it to her neck or otherwise directly threaten her. "You don't have much of a choice, Sebastian. You have been challenged. It is dishonorable to refuse. Nor, I think, do you want me to take this sword to one of these bookwyrms or to the sapling."

Viola's heart hammered even harder in her throat. "If you hurt me, the bookwyrms, or the sapling, it would be an act of war against the Court of Knowledge."

"Ah, yes, that is correct." Lord Chauvlyn sauntered yet another step closer. "But you see, the Court of Revels and Court of Knowledge are already at war, and they have been for the past twelve days."

Everything in her twisted tight. Her family. Her Court. They were in danger.

That would explain why the Anywhere Doors had locked tight. It must have something to do with the war, though Viola didn't know all the magic that must be involved.

Sebastian. Would Brigid know to look for him? Would he be able to find his way out of the between if all of the Anywhere Doors were locked and the courts were at war?

She'd have to worry about her family later. Right now, she had to figure out how to protect herself and the sapling.

With the courts at war, most of the usual protections no longer applied. She would have to fight Lord Chauvlyn.

Now would have been a good time to actually be Sebastian and have his years of training. All she had was a few cursory lessons from years ago before she decided sword fighting wasn't for her.

Sure, she'd spent plenty of time fighting monsters. But it didn't take loads of skill to fend off monsters. Just a sturdy stick and tenacity.

But fighting a fae lord? That took training and skill. Neither of which she possessed.

She gestured to the shovel. "I don't have a sword. Surely it isn't honorable to duel someone who is only armed with a shovel."

Lord Chauvlyn's sword lowered a fraction, as if that had caught him off guard more than anything else she'd said so far. "The brother of the Wild Fae Primrose doesn't have a sword? I find that hard to believe."

For good reason. Sebastian probably had a pocket full of swords. But Viola had never carried a sword. She didn't have enough training to carry a weapon since she was more likely to hurt herself or a friend than adequately defend herself.

"I'm a librarian on a peaceful island. I didn't think a sword would be necessary." Viola tried to give a casual shrug. Like something Brigid would have done in this situation.

Then again, Brigid would've had a sword. And a plan to get herself out of here safe and sound.

Lord Chauvlyn sighed, as if this was a terrible bother, and he switched his sword to his left hand.

Viola lunged for the shovel, but before she had fully curled her fingers around the shovel's handle, Lord Chauvlyn's sword was inches from her neck. She froze, then slowly raised her hands.

Lord Chauvlyn shook his head, as if he wanted to roll his eyes but was too much of a fae lord for such a gesture. He reached into his pocket again and pulled out a second rapier. He held the rapier out to her hilt-first.

She had no choice but to slip her hand into the sword's guard, gripping the sword's balanced weight as Lord

Chauvlyn released it. So far, Lord Chauvlyn hadn't seen through the glamour, but would he suspect once she began fighting? Well, flailing about with her sword would be more accurate.

If she thought Lord Chauvlyn would go easier on her if he knew she was Viola instead of Sebastian, she'd drop the glamour. But Lord Chauvlyn had proven he wasn't above hurting women and children. She was still safer as Sebastian than as herself.

Drawing in a deep breath, she stood and faced Lord Chauvlyn, trying to remember the sword stances she had been taught.

Lord Chauvlyn lunged, and Viola stumbled back, swinging her sword wildly. She totally missed Lord Chauvlyn and his sword, half-spinning with the force of her whiff.

The bookwyrms slithered out of the way, still hissing and growling.

Viola scrambled backwards, trying to keep out of the reach of Lord Chauvlyn's sword. When he stabbed at her, she couldn't help but give a shriek that was definitely unmanly. If Lord Chauvlyn hadn't already started to see through the glamour, he would soon.

Lord Chauvlyn lunged again, and Viola shrieked and dodged. Her back bumped into something, and she nearly fell. She was pinned against a bookcase with nowhere else to go.

Yet Lord Chauvlyn didn't press his advantage. Instead, he reached into a pocket—a different pocket this time—and pulled out a stoppered vial. He halted next to the silver-covered sapling, which was now waist-high.

The four bookwyrms hissed. Curio lunged and sank his

teeth into Lord Chauvlyn's ankle. Little puffs of smoke and flame snorted through his nose.

Lord Chauvlyn swore and kicked Curio, trying to dislodge him.

Belch and Toby shared a glance, then they launched themselves at Lord Chauvlyn with matching snarls. They latched onto his ankles, biting their way up his calves.

Swearing, dancing, and trying to beat them off with the hilt of his rapier, Lord Chauvlyn still didn't let go of the vial.

Viola gathered herself and forced herself forward on shaking legs, lifting the rapier. She didn't know what was in the vial, but it couldn't be good. She stabbed with the sword, but even though he had seemed distracted with the bookwyrms, Lord Chauvlyn still brought his sword up and flicked her sword aside.

Feste gathered herself and struck at Lord Chauvlyn. This time, he kicked the bookwyrm hard enough that the bookwyrm flew through the air and smashed into the nearest bookshelf. The bookwyrm yelped, collapsing to the floor with a whimper.

Viola clutched the rapier's hilt in a white-knuckled fist. That was enough. Lord Chauvlyn had hurt one of the bookwyrms.

With a yell, she rushed forward, swinging her sword with all the strength in her shoulders and arms.

Lord Chauvlyn parried her strikes, not even stumbling back under the meager force of her blows.

With his other hand, he popped the stopper off. Even as the bookwyrms crawled higher, biting and growling, and Viola slashed the rapier with all her might, he dumped the vial over the sapling. Black sludge drooled over the leaves, which shriveled and blackened.

"No!" Viola's grip on the sword loosened just a fraction as her heart sank. Her shock was only momentary, but it was enough. Lord Chauvlyn did something with his wrist and sword and next thing she knew, the rapier flew from her fingers, then clattered to the paving stones.

Viola staggered back, then crashed to her knees by the sapling, heedless of Lord Chauvlyn's sword.

He was too busy with the bookwyrms to try anything. He dropped his sword and grabbed Toby by the back of the neck, plucking him from his legs and tossing him away from him. "That's a poison. The tree in the Great Library is too large and magical to be susceptible. But this sapling isn't."

Lord Chauvlyn grimaced as he tore Curio off his thigh. The bookwyrm hissed, twisted, and puffed tongues of flame, trying to either bite or burn Lord Chauvlyn's hand. Lord Chauvlyn threw the bookwyrm, and Curio crashed into a bookshelf with a whine.

Viola reached for the sword again, wishing she was strong enough to defend the bookwyrms. They weren't big enough to fight off Lord Chauvlyn. They were supposed to protect the library from things like small monsters or rodents. Not fae lords.

"Right now, the sapling is drawing on the Library's Tree to grow this fast and bring the life of the Library into this outpost." Lord Chauvlyn probably would have been smirking, if he hadn't been trying to tear Belch off his calf. "The sapling will keep drawing the life of the Tree, trying to survive the poison. Maybe the Tree will survive and still grow the sapling, though it will severely weaken the Library. Or both this sapling and the Tree of the Great Library will die, killed by this poison. Either way, my king will take advantage of the weakness. Even now, he will be staging an attack."

Viola glanced from Lord Chauvlyn to the tree. The blackness of the sludge was growing, consuming more and more of the tree, even as silver kept gathering. More magic, drawing from the life of the Great Library itself, trying to keep the sapling alive.

She'd given Lord Chauvlyn this chance. Perhaps she shouldn't have planted the sapling. She should have waited for another chance to establish the outpost. It would have meant letting this sapling die and risk breaking the agreement between King Theseus and Duke Orsino regarding the Library. But it might have been better than this.

She hadn't realized that Lord Chauvlyn could use the sapling to poison the Great Library.

Lord Chauvlyn yanked Belch from his leg, chucking the snarling wyrm.

Belch tumbled on the paving stones but shook himself off, belching gouts of angry flames. Curio and Toby were slithering back toward Lord Chauvlyn, their eyes slitted, smoke curling from their nostrils. Even Feste had gotten up and stalked Lord Chauvlyn.

Lord Chauvlyn brandished his sword at them. Damp spots were growing on several places on his trousers, showing that the bookwyrms had left their mark on him. With his free hand, he patted at the flaming spots on his clothes, which were quickly doused by his blood.

Still, Lord Chauvlyn's expression remained sneering and far too confident. After all, he'd gotten everything he wanted. All they could do at this point was annoy him, drawing a little bit of blood, while he killed the Great Library.

"Even with the Great Library weakened, King Oberon will never be able to defeat King Theseus and Queen Hippolyta." Viola closed her fingers around the sword's hilt.

Lord Chauvlyn's mouth curled. "That wasn't the only king I was referring to."

"Claudius? He's calling himself a king now?" Viola grimaced. Claudius was a fae who had kidnapped humans two years ago, intending to use them in a massive blood rite to destroy the Laws of Binding in the Fae Realm and tear the realms apart. But he wasn't a king. He was just a lord from the Court of Revels who had gotten himself banished for performing blood rites and trying to usurp King Oberon.

"Claudius will be a king, once he claims this island for his own." Lord Chauvlyn took another step back, keeping the bookwyrms back with jabs of his sword. "His armies are pouring through the rifts you tore as we speak. Between him and the monsters, Duke Orsino's paltry forces don't stand a chance. This island will be ours by morning."

No, no, no. Viola couldn't absorb his words. The peaceful beaches. The meandering paths between the sea grass. The friendly fae who hadn't bothered her at all for being human.

The dark-eyed duke who loved organization and wore such a solemn countenance, hiding his true warmth.

They would all be hurt—or even killed—tonight because of the war between the Court of Revels and Court of Knowledge. Favian hadn't known what he was signing up for when he agreed to establish an outpost library.

There was nothing Viola could do to stop it. The sapling was already poisoned. The rifts were already open. Lord Chauvlyn had already won.

A rumble echoed through the palace a moment before the floor beneath his feet shuddered, sloshing juice over the rim of the glass in his hand.

What was that? Favian glanced around the room. His guests had all frozen where they were standing, glancing around much as he was.

Another tremor. Then a crash. The doors at the far end of the ballroom burst open, and a hydra slunk inside, its five heads hissing and snapping at the people closest to it.

How had the hydra gotten in? What was it doing here?

Questions for later. Right now, he needed to deal with the problem.

At least Viola wasn't here. She and her brother had left a few minutes ago, heading for the outpost library. She should be safe.

"Guards!" Favian plunged his hand into his pocket and drew out the sword he'd stashed there. He didn't wear a sword on his hip. There had been no need on his peaceful island. But after the warning from Sebastian about Lord Chauvlyn, Favian had taken to stowing a sword in his magical pocket.

Several of his guards converged on the hydra, batting at its heads. They didn't try to behead any of them. To kill a hydra, one had to either cut off all the heads at the exact same time or stab through its thick hide to its heart.

"Cesario!" Favian cast about for his steward.

All around him, the party guests screamed and stampeded in the opposite direction of the hydra.

"Yes, my lord." Cesario popped out of the crowd, appearing at Favian's elbow.

"Get everyone who will listen to the inner rooms of the palace." Favian gestured in that direction.

At only three feet tall, Cesario wasn't the most imposing or commanding of personages. The panicked people might not even notice him.

But Cesario just bowed and hurried off without question. He began shouting, his voice high-pitched but piercing enough to rise above the screams.

More of Favian's guards rushed to him, surrounding him. "Your Grace, you should get to safety."

"No, I can't leave." Favian took in the ballroom, his grip already going sweaty on his sword's hilt. While he'd trained with his guards, he'd never fought so much as a small monster before. Melyria generally stayed out of the chaos of the rest of the Fae Realm.

Somehow, Cesario was corralling the guests toward the doors to the inner corridors of the palace. It was mostly servants' quarters, kitchens, and storage rooms, leaving the rooms with the view for the duke, the guests, and the more public spaces.

His guards fended off the hydra heads while two rushed forward. One plunged his sword at the hydra's chest, only managing to get the tip of the sword into the hydra's tough scales. The second guard swung a mallet, driving the sword into the hydra's chest to the hilt.

The hydra flailed and screeched, even as blood poured from the wound. The guards jumped back as the hydra collapsed, roiling for a moment on the floor.

Even as the hydra died, a pack of large rodent creatures swarmed over the body, snarling at the guards.

But worse was the view through the double doors, no longer blocked by the hydra. Against the moonlight, a swirling, gaping black rift opened above the palace steps, disgorging even more monsters onto his island.

The hydra hadn't been a single monster that somehow got through. A rift to the Realm of Monsters had opened up, and now his island was under attack. Even as he stood there, gaping, another black tear sliced through the night by the cliff above the beach.

Viola. She was in danger.

"Keep the monsters from getting far from those rifts. Send a squad to the town." Favian pointed at the double doors, even as he turned and sprinted for the doors on the other side of the room, the ones closest to the outer doors leading to the back garden and outpost library. "I need to see to the librarians."

"My lord! Wait!" Several guards raced to keep up with him, but he didn't slow to let them catch up.

He ran through the corridors, then flung open the doors to the back garden. As he stepped into the night, the screams of frightened people and the screeches of monsters slammed into him. In the center of the garden, another rift tore across the night, disgorging a flood of harpies.

Favian gritted his teeth, flexed his fingers on his sword, then charged into the garden.

Two of the harpies swooped at him. He stabbed upward blindly, holding an arm above his head to try to protect his face. Claws tugged at his coat, then swiped across his chest, tearing his shirt and into his skin. Pain burned across his chest.

He stabbed upward again, and this time he must have hit something. One of the harpies screeched, flapping upward out of his reach. Splashes of hot blood landed on his head and shoulder.

Ugh. Battles were definitely not logical or organized. And very, very messy.

The other harpy clamped its claws on his sword arm, digging in its talons.

Favian cried out, but the harpy had a firm hold of his sword arm. It flapped its wings, lifting Favian from his feet. He punched his fist into the bird's belly, but its feathers seemed to absorb the blow so that it didn't so much as flinch.

Then his guards were there, stabbing the bird.

Favian squeezed his eyes shut as blood sprayed. The harpy dropped him, and he fell, landing hard on the ground. His arm throbbed, but he rolled back to his feet, still gripping his sword.

He had to get to Viola. What if a rift had opened up in the outpost library? Sure, her brother had training and could protect her. But Favian couldn't relax until he saw that she was safe.

THE DOOR to the outpost slammed open, and bootsteps pounded on the paving stones.

Viola picked up the sword and whirled, facing the aisle closest to the door. What now? What other enemy would she have to face?

Lord Chauvlyn spun too, so he must not be sure if this would be a friend or foe to him either. Yet he didn't spin all the way so that he could keep an eye on the four bookwyrms.

Favian raced around the corner of the nearest bookshelf. He gripped a sword, his white shirt torn and bloody beneath the dark green coat. His trousers, too, were spattered with grime. He skidded to a halt, taking in the scene, before he pointed his sword at Lord Chauvlyn. "What kind of attack is this? You're a guest on my island."

"Not officially. I sneaked onto the island and haven't been offered any hospitality." Lord Chauvlyn gave a slight bow to Favian. "I will take my leave. I need to meet my king."

Without waiting for Favian's response, Lord Chauvlyn spun on his heel and disappeared into one of the aisles between the curving shelves. Curio and Toby slithered after him, still puffing tongues of fire.

Favian ignored Lord Chauvlyn and marched toward Viola instead, though he only lowered his sword marginally.

She gestured to the doorway. "Claudius—"

"Where is Viola?" Favian cast about wildly, barely glancing at her.

Right. She still looked like Sebastian.

"Favian, I—" She reached to pull the pendant from

underneath her blouse. It was time to reveal the glamour and tell him what was really going on.

"I need to find her. The island is being attacked." Favian raced off, waving vaguely behind him. "Stay here and protect the sapling."

"But I…" Viola sighed as Favian disappeared around the corner. She glanced over her shoulder at the sapling. She couldn't leave it. The blackened section was growing, even as it pulsed with a silver, inner glow.

Feste and Belch, the two bookwyrms who hadn't chased after Lord Chauvlyn, slithered to her side and joined her in regarding the tree.

She rested her free hand on Feste. "Do you have any ideas? Because I don't."

Feste gave a mournful whine and snuggled closer into her hand. Her fingers came away with a few drops of blue bookwyrm blood.

Perhaps Viola should just yank the sapling up by the roots. Or chop it down with the sword. Would that be enough to kill it and sever the connection to the Tree in the Great Library?

But what if either of those actions harmed the Tree? How was she to know? She hadn't even known that it was possible to poison the Tree through the sapling.

She couldn't simply do nothing. That would certainly hurt the Great Library.

What if she simply pruned the tree? She had helped her parents with pruning, back when her family had a few fruit trees on their farm before the drought.

It had been a long time ago, but some things one didn't forget, no matter how long she had been off the farm and working in the Great Library.

She gripped the rapier in both hands, raised it above the tree, and brought it down on the infected branch.

The sword bit into the tree but didn't fully sever the branch. She had to hack at the branch several more times before it snapped off.

"Burn that, will you?" She tossed the branch onto one of the paving stones several feet away from the sapling.

The two bookwyrms slithered to the branch and puffed flames at it. Since the branch was green and the bookwyrms couldn't generate more than a small but hot flame, it took them some work to get it to burn.

Viola continued to hack at the tree, chopping off the twigs and branches that had been touched by the black sludge, tossing each of them onto the pyre the bookwyrms were burning.

Once she had all the branches lopped off and she couldn't find so much as a dot of sludge left, she dropped the sword and dug into the pocket of her librarian coat. Surely she had some tool she could use for pruning.

The poor sapling had only a few twigs and leaves left, looking decidedly sad and ragged. Had she chopped too much? Would it survive? Or, worse, would it draw too much from the Great Library in trying to survive?

Her fingers closed around what felt like a heavy-duty pair of shears, used in the Great Library for cutting leather for re-binding books. She pulled it out of her pocket, then tackled the broken ends left by the sword. The shears were sharp, and they sliced through the green sapling easily.

A few silver flakes drifted around the tree, moving sluggishly, as if the sapling was hovering between life and death.

When she had cleaned up the last stub of branch, Viola sat back on her heels, holding her breath, unable to tear her gaze away from the sapling. Would it pull through? Or had it lost too many branches too traumatically?

The pile of branches she'd cut off was nothing but a dusting of ashes, and the bookwyrms slithered with weary twists of their bodies as they returned to her side.

She drew them into her lap and hugged them close as they kept vigil over the sapling.

Chapter Sixteen

Sebastian gripped Olivia's hand as they raced through the town, winding through the streets upward toward the palace.

From somewhere ahead, someone screamed. Then a pack of shrieking fae raced toward Sebastian and Olivia, shouting something about a monster.

Sebastian switched hands with Olivia so that he was now holding her hand with his left. He reached into his pocket and drew out his sword, a heavier sword rather than the thin rapier that Brigid tended to prefer. "Stick close. Things are about to get messy."

A few more fae raced by. Then, a wolf the size of a pony bounded around the corner, its eyes glowing red and its jaws dripping foam.

What Sebastian wouldn't give to have his brother-in-law Munch at his back with his iron-tipped arrows and archery skills.

All Sebastian had was his sword. He released Olivia's hand, then raced forward to meet the wolf. He dodged the snapping jaws and plunged the sword into the wolf's chest.

The wolf kept snapping at him and trying to claw him, using its weight to bowl Sebastian over. It was all he could do to keep his hold of the sword.

A battle cry that rose into a shriek came from somewhere above him, then splinters of wood rained down onto the cobblestones around him.

Sebastian craned his neck, catching sight of Olivia's shoes and skirt a few feet away. "Run!"

She didn't. Instead, she held her ground, gripping the remains of a piece of wood in both hands.

Sebastian yanked out the sword and swung it at the wolf's neck.

More blood. A yelp. The wolf staggered, then dropped. Sebastian stabbed several more times for good measure, not stopping until the wolf fell completely still.

Sebastian met Olivia's gaze over the top of the dead wolf. She stood there, eyes wide, still gripping the piece of wood she'd broken over the wolf's head.

Then she dropped the wood, shook herself, and reached a hand to him.

He took her hand, and they jogged up the road once again, heading for the palace.

They ran into several more groups of fae being chased by monsters, and they had to take the long way around at one point when the road ahead of them split with a rift.

As they neared the palace, the sounds of fighting grew louder. Two groups of fae appeared to be battling each other.

"What's going on? Who are all these fae?" Olivia ran closer to him, her eyes wide.

"I don't know." Sebastian skirted around the palace. While he'd like to help Duke Orsino's guards, he couldn't bring Olivia into the middle of a battle. Nor would Duke Orsino's men recognize Sebastian. They'd likely see his sword dripping blood and assume he was the enemy.

Whatever was going on, it seemed he had stepped from one war zone into another.

Right now, he just wanted to find Viola and get her and Olivia onto Captain Antonio's ship. Once he was sure they were safe, he would return and see how he could help.

They sneaked through the gardens surrounding the palace, doing their best to avoid fleeing fae, fighting guards, and snarling monsters.

The outpost library lay just ahead, bathed in a wash of silver moonlight that seemed far too beautiful and serene for this night of blood.

As he placed a foot on the step, a figure dressed in black burst out of the double doors, a sword in his hand. But he skidded to a halt, his eyes widening. More puzzled than anything.

"Lord Chauvlyn." Sebastian raised his sword. "I should have known you would be behind this."

"Didn't I just..." Lord Chauvlyn trailed off, glancing behind him to where both of the doors still stood open, giving a gaping view into the outpost library and the first spirals of shadowed shelves. Then his jaw firmed, and he raised his sword again. "Let me pass, unless you want a rematch. It seems your sword skills were exaggerated. You didn't acquit yourself so well in our first bout."

First bout? Sebastian hadn't...

Viola. Must have been. Was she all right?

No time to think about that now. He just had to get to her.

Sebastian couldn't let Lord Chauvlyn put the pieces together. He raised his sword and faced the fae lord. "You took me by surprise earlier. You won't find my skills so paltry now."

Lord Chauvlyn's jaw worked, eyes flashing, before he lunged into a sword strike, using his height at the top of the stairs to his advantage to press Sebastian back.

Sebastian parried easily, dancing backward a few paces to force Lord Chauvlyn to come down the steps toward him. Once they were both on level ground, he pressed forward. He had to get into the outpost, and he didn't dare let Lord Chauvlyn get past him where the fae lord could hurt Olivia. Or use her as a hostage against him.

Lord Chauvlyn also parried, but he didn't seem as sprightly on his feet as usual. In the moonlight, it was difficult to tell, but slightly darker patches stained his black clothes. Still, he was a fae lord, and he was skilled.

With each blow and parry, Lord Chauvlyn's eyes widened, a furrow forming across his brow. If he fought Viola earlier, thinking she was Sebastian, then he must be puzzled at Sebastian's sudden change in sword fighting skills.

As Sebastian lunged again, He forced Lord Chauvlyn backward up the steps. Lord Chauvlyn stumbled, off balance and flailing for a moment as he scrambled to find his footing. Sebastian pressed him yet another step back, and Lord Chauvlyn grabbed one of the doors to steady himself as he clumsily parried.

Two bookwyrms slithered around the corner of the last row of shelves inside the outpost library. With matching growls, they launched themselves through the open doorway at Lord Chauvlyn's ankles.

He gave a snarl of his own, muttering something like *Not again* as he tried to fend off Sebastian and the bookwyrms.

Sebastian knocked Lord Chauvlyn's sword aside, then grabbed his sword wrist, pressing his own sword to the fae lord's throat. "Drop your sword."

Lord Chauvlyn grimaced at Sebastian—or perhaps at the pain from the bookwyrms gnawing on his ankles. The muscles in his wrist flexed beneath Sebastian's hand, as if he were thinking about trying to pull free.

Inside the outpost library, another figure raced around the bookshelves, sword in hand. Duke Orsino halted in the open doorway, his eyes widening as he glanced from Sebastian to Lord Chauvlyn. But after a moment, he raised his sword, pointing at the fae lord. "I suggest you do as he says."

Lord Chauvlyn's jaw worked, but he released his grip on his sword. It fell, clattering, onto the stone steps, sliding down until it landed with a clunk against the gravel path of the garden.

Olivia hurried forward, grabbed Lord Chauvlyn's sword, then backed away again.

Sebastian risked sending her a nod before he slid his own sword back into his magical pocket. While the sword was grimy now, it would be perfectly clean when he pulled it out again. Then he twisted Lord Chauvlyn's arm behind his back. "I claim you as a prisoner of the Court of Knowledge in our war with the Court of Revels."

Lord Chauvlyn's sneer was more a snarl, but he didn't protest with words. He was well and truly caught, and now he'd been bound in a captive binding. There was little he could do.

As soon as Sebastian placed the captive binding on Lord Chauvlyn, the bookwyrms stopped chewing on the fae lord's ankles. They slithered back, still snarling with their ruffs puffed out to make them appear bigger.

Duke Orsino's gaze snapped to Sebastian. "The Court of Knowledge and the Court of Revels are at war? You didn't mention this earlier."

Because Viola, who had apparently been walking around with Sebastian's face, didn't know yet, unless Lord Chauvlyn had told her. The fae lord hadn't started at Sebastian's pronouncement of a war, so he must have been forewarned by his king when he'd been sent here for nefarious purposes.

"The news came with the ship that just docked in the harbor." Not a lie. Just not the whole truth.

Though now might be the time to start revealing the truth. Once Sebastian figured out what that whole truth was.

Another burst of screams rang from the direction of the castle. Duke Orsino tightened his grip on his sword.

Lord Chauvlyn's gaze swept from the outpost library to the palace. "It doesn't matter if you know now or not. I have accomplished my mission. It is too late for you."

"We'll see about that." Duke Orsino started to brush past Lord Chauvlyn and Sebastian. "Stay here and guard the library, your prisoner, and Olivia. I need to find Viola. She's not inside."

"Actually, I believe she is." Sebastian nudged Lord Chauvlyn up the stairs.

"I just searched the place. She isn't in there." Duke

Orsino's eyes flashed, more emotion twisting his face than Sebastian had ever seen from the fae duke.

Hmm. Duke Orsino seemed strangely fixated on finding Viola. How close had the duke and Sebastian's sister gotten in the past twelve days?

Perhaps Sebastian should let Duke Orsino rush off trying to find Viola. Or go protect his island from the invasion of fae and monsters like a good fae duke should.

But Sebastian had a gut feeling that the answers to all of this lay not out there but inside the outpost library with Viola. They all needed to compare notes and figure out what had been going on in both places before they could solve anything.

Sebastian dug into his pocket, pulled out a length of the sturdy cord used for binding books, and tied Lord Chauvlyn's hands behind his back. "I think we should look again. Trust me. She's in there."

Duke Orsino scowled at him, but he spun on his heel and marched back the way he'd come.

Sebastian kept one hand gripping Lord Chauvlyn's arm, but he reached for Olivia with his free hand.

She glanced from Duke Orsino's retreating back to Sebastian. She lifted her chin, then took Sebastian's hand, her fingers tightening around his as if determined to never let him go.

He wasn't ever going to let her go either. It was time for all truths to be revealed. Including the truth about him and Olivia.

FAVIAN FLEXED his fingers on his sword. Where was Viola? Rogue fae and slavering monsters were roaming his island, and Viola was nowhere to be found.

Then there was Sebastian. How had the man gotten from the center of the outpost library to outside of the library before Favian? Sure, the curving shelves were a bit of a maze. But not that much. He certainly shouldn't have had enough time to have a whole sword fight with Lord Chauvlyn.

On top of all that, what had he been doing with Olivia? What was Olivia even doing here? She hadn't been at the party, despite being invited. He'd hoped she'd come. Hoped he'd have a chance to pull her aside and finally talk.

But then she hadn't been there, and he'd escorted Viola and forgot about everything and everyone else.

More shouts and screams pierced the night and his heart. He should be out there with his people, defending his island.

But not until he found Viola and made sure she was safe. The thought of her out there in the night, alone and surrounded by monsters, sent such a crawling, tight feeling up into his throat.

He wound through the curving library shelves, only vaguely registering the footfalls of Lord Chauvlyn, Sebastian, and Olivia behind him. The two bookwyrms slithered on either side of them, as if they believed Lord Chauvlyn was their prisoner.

The silvery glow brightened up ahead. Glittering silver dust seemed to drift through the beams of moonlight, spreading out to land on the surrounding shelves.

As Favian strode around the final curve and into the

center space of the outpost library, he had to squint into the moonlight at the figure kneeling beside the tree.

Unlike the blackened sapling he'd left behind, the tree was now as tall as he was, bursting outward and shedding silver sparkles. Roots were flowing through the ground while the surrounding shelves were bursting with flowers and leaves and life that hadn't been there moments ago.

The figure stood and faced them.

Sebastian.

But…Favian spun. Sebastian was still frog-marching a bound Lord Chauvlyn, Olivia at their heels. Sebastian and Olivia were still mostly hidden in the shadows, but Favian was close enough to make them out.

Two Sebastians. What was going on?

The Sebastian by the tree planted his hands on his hips. "As you can see, Lord Chauvlyn, you didn't win. At least not when it comes to the tree. You forgot. I grew up on a farm. I know how to prune a tree in a pinch."

Lord Chauvlyn's jaw worked again, but he didn't respond. His eyes didn't flash. Instead, he had a kind of resigned look, as if he'd figured out exactly what was going on and where he had gone wrong.

The Sebastian guarding Lord Chauvlyn pushed the fae lord another step forward, bringing both of them fully into the light from the rapidly growing tree.

The Sebastian by the tree gasped, swaying a step forward. "Sebastian?"

The Sebastian with Lord Chauvlyn released the fae lord, stepping to one side. "Are you all right?"

"You're alive." The other Sebastian had tears trickling down his face. And something about him seemed to be… flickering? Almost appearing a bit Viola-like.

Favian squeezed his eyes shut and shook his head, trying to clear his vision. By the time he opened his eyes again, the two Sebastians were embracing. One crying, the other speaking in low tones.

The not-crying Sebastian reached to the back of the other's neck and lifted up something on a string.

As soon as he did, the image of the other Sebastian blurred, then disappeared, leaving Viola standing there, hugging her brother and crying.

A glamour. But why would Viola be wearing a glamour and pretending to be her brother?

How long had this been going on? First Olivia not speaking to him, and now Viola using a glamour.

Why were all the women in Favian's life so reluctant to have an honest discussion with him?

Chapter Seventeen

Favian braced himself against the shelves behind him, trying to take it all in. He couldn't even process enough words to ask for an explanation.

"Sebastian? What's going on?" Olivia still held Lord Chauvlyn's sword, pointing it vaguely in the fae lord's direction. But her gaze was darting between Sebastian and Viola.

Favian wanted to know that answer too. He just wasn't sure his heart was ready to hear it.

Sebastian stepped back out of Viola's embrace, then turned so that he was facing everyone.

Viola peeked at Favian briefly before she focused on Olivia. "Sebastian didn't make it through the Anywhere Door the day I arrived. It was just me. Something happened as we were stepping into it, and he pushed me so I fell through before the Door snapped shut. I wasn't sure what to do, so I used the glamour necklace my sister had given me to pretend to be both Sebastian and myself. I didn't know what was going on or who I could trust."

Favian sagged against the shelves behind him. For the past twelve days, any time he had spoken with Sebastian, he had really been speaking with Viola.

He understood why she might have decided not to tell him right away. But after they had started to get to know each other? Didn't she trust him?

Olivia blinked, her eyes widening. "Then every time I talked with Sebastian in the past few days…"

"It was really me." Viola winced. "Sorry about that. I wanted to tell you. I wanted to tell you all." She peeked at Favian again, something in her gaze pleading. "But then I found out Lord Chauvlyn was on the island. I didn't know what his plan was, but I knew I couldn't let him find out I was here alone."

Still, couldn't she have trusted Favian enough to tell him what was going on? Instead, she had come to him as Sebastian to ask for guards.

He had only known Viola for twelve days. Her lack of trust in him shouldn't hurt this much.

Olivia's forehead puckered, her eyes filling. "I thought Sebastian had said…but if that was you, then why did we…" She glanced at Sebastian—the real Sebastian—and made a twitching motion with her wrist.

Something glinted faintly in the moonlight and magic.

What was that? It almost looked like…

But that couldn't be. Surely Olivia wouldn't have…

His stomach sank further, and he might have staggered if he hadn't already been leaning against the shelves. He barely noticed as a branch sprouted next to his head, tickling his ear. A few truths of the past two years were becoming all too clear.

Viola's shoulders hunched even further. "I just wanted to

get you out of the way tonight, Olivia. I'm sorry I couldn't think of anything else, but Lord Chauvlyn threatened you. I didn't want you at your home or the outpost library or anywhere else Lord Chauvlyn might find you. I just thought you'd spend the night wandering the beach alone. You'd get your heart broken when Sebastian didn't show up, but you'd be safe."

"Except that I did show up." Sebastian sighed and shared a look with Olivia. "And I didn't know your plan except what Olivia told me. So I assumed...perhaps I wanted to assume..."

Lord Chauvlyn snorted, drawing all their gazes back to him. Favian had nearly forgotten that the fae lord was still standing there. But captive-bound as he was, he couldn't try to escape, even though their attention had strayed.

The fae lord's sneer had almost a wry tilt to it. "I knew the two of you would do something foolish if I threatened Lady Olivia enough. It turns out I only succeeded because of a coincidence. That's humiliating."

"For all of us." Sebastian grimaced and glanced at Olivia again. "I think it's time we told him."

Olivia, too, hunched, but she nodded before she turned to Favian. "I'm so sorry, Favian. This isn't how I wanted you to find out."

Favian squeezed his eyes shut. How could he have been so blind? So foolish? "These past two years when you've been avoiding me. It was because of him, wasn't it."

"Yes." Her voice was quiet, yet it held a note of regret. "I met Sebastian when I went to the Great Library to get away and clear my head after our fathers died. I went back several times over the next weeks, and he would recommend books that would keep my mind off the grief.

Sebastian lost his parents too, and we talked. And that helped."

"Then the outpost library? The only reason you pushed for it was because you wanted to bring Sebastian to the island." Favian couldn't help that his voice came out flat. A touch hard.

She'd told him the outpost library would make her happy. He'd thought he was doing it as a gift to her. She had implied that if he built the outpost library for her, she would start talking to him again.

But it had all been a lie. A trick to get her secret lover here to the island. All this time, she had been going behind his back.

And apparently it had been so obvious to everyone that Lord Chauvlyn had seen it within days of arriving on the island.

He was a fool. A humiliated fool.

And he'd thought he and Olivia were friends. That they cared about each other.

"Why didn't you just tell me, Olivia?" Favian still couldn't bring himself to look at her. He leaned his head back against the shelf behind him. "We grew up together. We were like family. You could have been honest with me."

"Could I? You became so hard, so driven after our fathers died." Olivia's voice cracked at that last word. "Fulfilling the bargain was all you could talk about. Every time I brought it up—tried to bring up that we could research a way out of it—you shut me down. Eventually, I gave up. Perhaps going behind your back wasn't the right way to handle this, but I wasn't sure what else to do."

"So this is all my fault?" Favian couldn't help the bite to his tone. Perhaps it was petty, lashing out at her. He had been hard after his father's death. Only in the past few days with Viola had he finally started to feel like himself again.

But he'd been grieving while doing his best to protect an entire island.

"No, not your fault. Just…" Olivia trailed off, then drew in a shuddering breath. "I didn't want to hurt you, Favian. You're right. You're family. But that's just it. You're like a brother to me. I couldn't see myself marrying someone I saw as a brother. And if you stop to think, you'll see I'm like a sister to you. You don't really want to marry me any more than I wanted to marry you."

Favian released a long sigh. That was the worst part. She was right. He'd only wanted to marry Olivia because he had no choice thanks to the bargain. He'd told himself they would be all right because they were fond of each other. Maybe they would have been.

But it would have merely been all right. Merely been a vague fondness.

He'd never been tempted to kiss Olivia while walking along the beach at sunset. He'd never found himself so eager to spend time with her that he dropped all his duties to pour over incomprehensible poetry.

No, when he contemplated kissing and smiling and laughing and avoiding his duties, he saw Viola, not Olivia.

Sure, he didn't know how deep his attraction to Viola went after a mere twelve days. But he had never been attracted to Olivia this way no matter how much time he spent with her.

"This is all very touching." Lord Chauvlyn's sneering baritone sliced through the moment. "While it seems my mission to weaken the Great Library's tree was thwarted, I still succeeded in opening rifts onto your island. My king will be here shortly, and I suggest that you prepare to surrender to him. You will not wish to find out what he does to those who resist."

Favian finally forced his eyes open and pushed away from the bookshelf.

Sebastian gripped Lord Chauvlyn's arm, giving him a slight shake. "You keep your mouth shut. You've caused enough trouble."

Lord Chauvlyn shut his mouth, but that sneering smirk had returned to his face. Once this was all over, Favian might ask for the Court of Knowledge's permission to punch their prisoner. Not that he was usually given to punching, and he'd probably hurt his hand doing it, but it would be worth it.

Yet the fae lord had a point. The rifts to the Realm of Monsters had been opened, unleashing destruction on Favian's island. And there was nothing he could do about it. His guards weren't equipped to stop the horde of monsters, much less an invading army.

Viola was still hugging her arms to her, almost too conspicuously not looking at Favian. "He's talking about Claudius, not King Oberon."

Sebastian frowned, his shoulders slumping. "We'd be better off if it was King Oberon. He's a fool."

"Yes. Fool enough to align himself with an evil fae who once tried to usurp his throne." Viola, too, frowned, glancing over her shoulder at the tree. "At least the tree seems to be doing all right, so the Court of Knowledge should be safe. As for the island, is there any way to close the rifts?"

Sebastian glanced at Olivia, then turned to Favian. "Most

rifts can be closed if whatever broken binding that caused the rift is repaired."

Favian crossed his arms and glared at Sebastian. "You and Olivia are the ones who broke the bargain and caused the rifts. Do you have any ideas for fixing this?"

Perhaps it was harsh. But he was the injured party here, and he wasn't feeling all that forgiving at the moment.

Sebastian held Favian's gaze without flinching. Not backing down, but also not angry. "For the past months, I've been researching ways to get out of bargains lawfully without breaking them."

"We wanted to do this right. But tonight…" Olivia flapped a hand in the air on a sigh. "Well, it seemed like the right thing at the time. Lord Chauvlyn was threatening me, and we were hoping true love would be enough."

"It clearly wasn't." Favian wasn't ready to let this go just yet. Not to mention that he had better things to do than stand here talking. Such as defend his island from the monsters unleashed from the rift.

"The one way I found to get out of a bargain involving a marriage like this is a substitute." Sebastian met Olivia's gaze. "A substitute would have to agree to take Olivia's place in the bargain. Preferably a family member or friend. The close relationship seems to be important for the magic to count the person as a substitute."

Olivia frowned. "I don't have any close family members. Or many friends. Unless my maid Marie would count?"

Favian struggled to hold back his own frown. Marie was hardly a suitable substitute.

But if he was understanding this correctly…perhaps it didn't necessarily have to be *Olivia's* family.

His heart pounded harder. Not with fear. Or anger. Could this squeezing in his throat possibly be *hope*?

Favian held Sebastian's gaze, not daring to so much as glance at Viola. "Librarian Sebastian, you—and thus your family—are the ones who broke the bargain and snatched Olivia. Thus it should be up to your family to provide restitution in the form of a substitute."

Sebastian's jaw worked, even as his blue eyes glinted with an edge. "No. Absolutely not."

How had Favian missed seeing through the glamour? Now that he saw them together, there was no mistaking Sebastian's mannerisms for Viola's. She had done her best, but she couldn't quite exude the big brother, I-will-beat-you-up-if-you-touch-my-sister menace that Sebastian was giving him now.

"Why not?" Favian eyed him, finding that his anger over Sebastian's and Olivia's actions was fading. "Shouldn't that be up to her?"

For the first time in two years, he was free. He could choose. And he was making his choice.

Now he could only hope that she would make the same choice.

VIOLA GASPED, pressing her hands over her mouth, as she gaped at Favian. Was he saying what she thought he was saying?

Favian turned to her, his dark brown eyes liquid and bright with an emotion she couldn't name. "Viola, I know this is sudden. But we wouldn't have to marry right away.

We would have time to…to get to know each other better. Please, take Olivia's place in the bargain. Save my island."

Sebastian, too, turned to her. "You don't have to do this, Viola. We can find another substitute. I will not have you trapped now that I've finally freed Olivia."

Favian glowered at Sebastian. "I'm not some monster to be avoided."

"You aren't. But the bargain is." Sebastian glared right back.

"Stop it, both of you." Viola scowled at each of them before she squeezed her eyes shut, trying to buy herself a moment to think.

They didn't have time to find another substitute. She could close the rifts right now if she just agreed.

Perhaps they could find a different substitute, once this was all over. She could agree just as a temporary measure.

Did she want to do that? This was what she'd wanted, wasn't it? This was her chance to claim Favian for herself.

Besides, she didn't want to do to him what Olivia had. He was too good, too honorable. He deserved to have someone take on the bargain who was as dedicated to fulfilling it as he was.

Viola faced Favian and drew in a deep breath.

Sebastian must have read something in her face. He stepped forward, reaching for her. "Viola, you don't—"

"Sebastian, I know what I'm doing." Viola shot her brother a look.

He halted, hand in the air, his mouth flapping for a moment.

It was the first time Viola had disagreed with her brother like this. With anyone in her family, really.

She never would have made a stand like this before these

past twelve days. But being thrown into this situation had taught her to think for herself. She was stronger than she'd ever realized.

Strong enough to take on a fae bargain and get exactly what she wanted out of the deal.

The relaxed smirk dropped from Lord Chauvlyn's face. He straightened and stepped forward, his own mouth opening as if he intended to interrupt.

Olivia kicked Lord Chauvlyn's ankle right where the bookwyrms had been gnawing earlier. Lord Chauvlyn gasped and stumbled back.

Viola shared a conspiratorial look with Olivia, then finally turned to Favian. Her heart beat harder at the look in his deep brown eyes. "Duke Favian Orsino, since my family broke the bargain, I agree to be the substitute and take Olivia's place."

As soon as she said the final word, a flare of magic brightened around each of them. Perhaps it was the tree, which was now spreading branches and leaves over the library near the ceiling.

But something snapped through the air, trembling through the ground beneath her feet. Was that a good tremble? Or another bad tremble?

Lord Chauvlyn huffed and slumped. "It is ridiculous how easy it is for your family to just skirt around the bindings whenever it is convenient for you."

"Hardly convenient." Sebastian gripped Lord Chauvlyn's arm again and gave him a small shake.

Viola shared one last look with Favian. With the deep frown lines digging grooves around his mouth, he didn't look particularly pleased with her agreement.

Had he only asked to save his island? He'd sounded like

he was bargaining for her, not just for his island. But how was she to know?

Favian spun away from her, waving back at them. "All of you, stay here. I need to see to my island."

Viola swiped the rapier she'd gotten from Lord Chauvlyn from the paving stones. "I'm coming with you."

Favian whirled back to her, his face as hard and frowning as she'd ever seen. "No."

His word was echoed by Sebastian behind her.

Ugh. She hadn't learned to stand on her own two feet just to have her decisions constantly questioned by both Favian and Sebastian. "I know I'm not much of a hand at sword fighting, but I've spent the past seven years defending the Great Library from monsters. I'm not entirely useless, especially if we're fighting monsters rather than fae. I'm bound to marry you now. This island is my island. Sebastian and Olivia will be more than enough to guard Lord Chauvlyn and the outpost library. I'm coming with you."

Favian opened his mouth, shut it, then nodded.

Viola hurried after Favian before her brother had a chance to protest. Besides, it was all Sebastian's fault that she had grown a backbone. He was the one, after all, who had talked her into coming, then left her here alone for twelve days.

She fell into step beside Favian, gripping the sword even though she had no intention of using it.

This was her place, and she had every intention of claiming it.

Chapter Eighteen

Favian strode through the outpost library, headed for the exit.

He'd need to have a conversation with Viola after this was all over. Preferably a private conversation. Somewhere romantic. Like the beach. Or the outpost library conveniently free of big brothers and former betrotheds.

Was this new bargain unwanted? What if Favian's attraction wasn't reciprocated? He didn't trust his feelings when it came to love. After all, look at the mess he'd made with Olivia. He hadn't seen how miserable she had been, and she hadn't even dared tell him that she didn't want to marry him.

He didn't want Viola to feel forced to marry him either. Would she want to avoid him too once she was a part of this bargain?

She certainly didn't seem reluctant at the moment, not with the way she was trotting at his side, rapier in hand.

He'd have to figure out whatever this was with Viola

later. Once the monsters were dead and his island was no longer in danger.

With sword in hand, he strode down the steps of the outpost and into the garden.

"Duke Orsino!" The voice came from closer to the ground, even as Favian's knee bumped into something.

Or someone.

"I'm sorry, Cesario." He reached down and steadied Cesario. The blue-skinned sprite was nearly invisible in the silver-blue darkness, and Favian had forgotten in his hurry to watch for those far shorter than him. "Report?"

"The guards have set up a perimeter around the palace. Squads have been deployed to the village to hunt down the monsters and the rogue fae." Cesario straightened, tugging at his clothes. His efforts did little good. His clothes were rumpled, torn, and stained with bits of dark blue blood. "The rifts were a problem, but they just closed a few seconds ago."

Good. Then at least Sebastian's research had been correct, and one problem had been fixed.

Favian resisted the urge to glance at Viola as he hurried down the path toward the palace. "Then let's finish this and take back our island."

Perhaps he wouldn't get a chance to punch Lord Chauvlyn. And likely not Sebastian either.

But Favian could channel his anger into killing fae monsters and rounding up the rogue fae so that they could be booted back to the Realm of Monsters where they had come from.

Together, he, Viola, and Cesario jogged along the paths, then along the palace's porch. The palace appeared free of monsters, and they had to go partway down the street to the village before they reached the line of his guards, fending off both a swarm of monsters and a squad of black-clad fae.

With a deep breath, Favian lunged forward, joining his guards as they fought the rogue fae.

Out of the corner of his eye, he caught sight of Viola. She joined a squad of the island villagers as they whacked at the monsters with a variety of kitchen implements, keeping them from attacking the guards from the rear. Viola swung her rapier more like a club than a sword, but it was still effective against the large rodents and skittering spiders.

He didn't have a chance to watch more because a fae was stabbing at him.

After this was all over, he and Viola needed a long, honest discussion. But until then, he was thankful to have her at his back.

FAVIAN STABBED his sword into yet another monster, ignoring the hot gush of blood. He was grimy. Blood-spattered. Sweaty. He had never been so gross in his life.

But as the chimera flopped over, gasping out its final breath, he glanced around and didn't see another monster charging toward him.

The warm glow of dawn spread along the horizon, bathing the blood-spattered streets with pink, as if trying to hide the carnage of the night.

He swiped the back of his sleeve across his forehead, but all he did was smear the blood and sweat around. He grimaced and dropped his arm.

Viola halted next to him. She, too, was grimy and blood-smeared. "That was the last of the monsters, at least in this area. Ugh. That was as bad as the fight a couple of years ago when King Oberon unleashed a horde of monsters on the Court of Knowledge."

"You mentioned this wasn't your first monster fight." Favian eyed his sword, running with monster blood and gore, then scrubbed the blade against his trousers. The trousers were a lost cause at this point.

"A hazard of living in a court that shares the Tanglewood with the Court of Revels. Midsummer nights were already chaotic even before King Oberon began actively allying himself with Claudius." Viola grimaced at her own sword before she slid it into a pocket. "Monsters are one thing. An army of rogue fae from the Realm of Monsters is another."

"Yes." Favian sighed, a weight settling heavy on his shoulders. While fighting the monsters had been bad, the rogue fae had been far worse. They were superior fighters to his guards, and only their limited numbers had kept them from completely overrunning the island. He and Viola must have gotten the rifts closed just in time before the bulk of the army from the Realm of Monsters could leap through.

Favian started to sheath his sword but froze as the sound of boots on the cobbles came from ahead of them. He whirled to face the street again, raising his sword once again.

Had more rogue fae come through the rifts? Favian had already lost far too many of his people trying to stop them. Were his remaining uninjured guards in any shape for yet another fight?

Was he up for another fight? After such a long night, all he wanted to do was bathe, then sleep for hours until he forgot that he would have to deal with all the death and destruction of this night.

As the group ahead rounded a corner and came into sight, Favian's weariness vanished in a wave of heat that squeezed his chest. This was worse than a gang of rogue fae. He stepped in front of Viola, shielding her. "Stand ready, men."

Around Favian, his guards readied their weapons again. Viola's shoes scuffed on the cobbles as she took a step back, whispering to the townsfolk who had become her little army during the long night.

Captain Antonio and his band of pirates halted a few yards away. They also held their weapons at the ready.

"What are you doing here? You were banished from the island." Favian stared at the face of the man who had killed his father. If only he could lunge forward and drive his sword into the man's chest.

But Captain Antonio was too light on his feet for that. Nor would the captain's pirate crew let Favian live if he tried such a thing. Not that Favian was the murdering type anyway, unlike the pirate before him.

Still, revenge was tempting.

"I brought Sebastian to find his sister." Captain Antonio lowered his sword. He didn't sheath it, likely because it was still dripping monster guts and needed a good cleaning before being put away. "When my crew and I saw all the trouble, we stepped in to help." Captain Antonio's tone softened. "I never killed your father, Duke Orsino."

"You were seen raiding the wreckage." Favian would have crossed his arms, but he was still holding his sword and he had no desire to lower it. He settled for glaring.

"Searching for your father's body, not for loot." Captain

Antonio sighed, his shoulders slumping. But he didn't look away as he would have if he had been lying. Instead, he held Favian's gaze steadily. "As I told you before. But I don't suppose you will listen to me now any more than you did back then."

There was a subtle accusation in those words, beneath the resignation. If Favian hadn't already been accused once that night of not listening, he might have brushed Captain Antonio off.

But Favian hadn't been listening to anyone back then, too wrapped up in his own grief. He'd hurt Olivia by not listening. Had he done the same thing to Captain Antonio?

For two years, he'd been convinced that Captain Antonio and his crew killed his and Olivia's fathers. But had he been wrong?

Today was a day for truth, now that he was finally ready to hear it.

Favian sighed and lowered his sword. "Stand down, men. Captain Antonio, would your men be willing to continue helping with the cleanup? You and I need to talk."

"Yes." Captain Antonio turned to his men and barked orders.

Favian gave a few orders of his own to his men. A few of them looked askance at Captain Antonio, but they didn't protest beyond a few mutters too low for Favian to overhear.

When Captain Antonio nodded, Favian set out along the winding street toward the palace. Viola fell into step with him, thankfully not saying anything. Captain Antonio followed, trailed by several of Favian's guards.

A few of the townsfolk peeked out of doors and windows, and Favian nodded to them, though he waved for them to remain inside. Until he had a chance to do a full sweep of the island to make absolutely sure that no rogue fae or monsters remained, it would be safer for his people to remain inside.

When he, Viola, and Captain Antonio reached the wide, columned porch, Favian halted and leaned a shoulder against a column. He was too grimy to want to so much as step foot in his study. And something was too wound up inside him to want to brave a confined space. The open space, the clean sea breezes, were exactly what he needed right now.

Viola touched his arm. "I'll leave the two of you to talk. I'd like to check on my brother and the outpost library."

Favian nodded, then motioned to his guards. Two of them trailed after Viola as she continued around the porch and into the back garden. From here, Favian could just see her as she disappeared safely into the outpost library.

Once she was safe, Favian forced himself to sheathe his sword. He didn't want to have this conversation while holding a weapon. It would be too tempting to use it, and he now suspected he would be targeting an innocent man. "You didn't kill my father."

Captain Antonio rested his back against a pillar, crossing his boots at the ankle as if he were relaxing in a comfortable chair instead of standing next to a pillar. "No."

Favian should have believed him two years earlier. He'd known Captain Antonio for years. Why would he have taken some other ship captain's word over Antonio's that day?

Because he'd been numb. Looking for someone to blame. And the other captain's testimony had been compelling, especially since Captain Antonio hadn't denied that he had been there.

It was time Favian listened now. "What happened that day?"

"My lookout caught a glimpse of something in the water, and we went to investigate." Captain Antonio shook his head, his gaze drifting away from Favian's to stare into the dawn without seeing. "We found a couple of bodies first, then wreckage of the ship. There were no survivors, but it looked like some of the bodies had been killed with weapons rather than from drowning."

The other captain had said the same thing, which was what had convinced Favian back then that Captain Antonio must have been the one to do it. He had a reputation as a pirate, though he'd never been accused of anything specific. He was merely unaffiliated with any court, which was basically the same thing as being a pirate here in the Fae Realm.

"We recovered a few of the bodies before the other ship came along and drove us off, convinced that we had been the ones to do it." Captain Antonio spread his hands, something in his stance pleading. "Your father was always willing to give me and my crew a berth here on Melyria. I would never have hurt him."

Favian squeezed his eyes shut for a moment, trying to banish the memory of his father's body, far too long dead and only semi-preserved in a barrel of brine. "I know. I should have believed you back then."

"With the evidence against me, I'm not sure I would have believed me either." Captain Antonio's smile was more sad than anything else. He didn't motion to his ears—his round, human ears—but the implication was there. Captain

Antonio was human. He wasn't well regarded here in the Fae Realm.

Favian wanted to believe that hadn't played into his decision to banish Captain Antonio. But had he subconsciously been more inclined to believe the fae sea captain over the human Captain Antonio?

"I've done some investigating of my own in the past two years." Captain Antonio scrubbed at the back of his neck. "I've never been able to pin down a culprit. But there have been growing rumors of a black ship that sails in and out of the realm through rifts to the Realm of Monsters. I don't know if the black ship belongs to Claudius or reports to him. It likely could be another band of rogue fae. The Realm of Monsters is filled with them."

Favian nodded, frowning. "But after the attack tonight, it isn't out of the realm of possibilities that Claudius would target the Island of Melyria."

"It seems highly suspicious to me that your father was killed shortly after the Court of Knowledge thwarted Claudius's attempt to round up humans to perform a massive blood rite and destroy the Laws of Bindings." Captain Antonio gestured, as if to indicate the island spreading out before them. "Claudius might have then decided to target your island as a good foothold in the Fae Realm."

"Father had mentioned he was worried about something, though he didn't tell me what it was." Favian wished his father had confided more before he'd died. Instead, Favian had been left floundering, young and alone. "I suspect he and Olivia's father thought they were protecting the island by making the bargain for me and Olivia to marry. While they always joked about the two of us marrying while we were growing up, they wouldn't have made it an official bargain without a good reason. It was just before they died that our fathers began pushing us regarding their bargain."

Instead of protecting the island, the bargain had given Claudius the perfect way to attack them. Although if Favian and Olivia had actually fallen in love, there wouldn't have been a problem.

Yet, Favian couldn't regret that he hadn't fallen in love with Olivia. She was right. Favian didn't feel for Olivia anything but brotherly affection. Nothing like what he felt for Viola, and he'd only known Viola twelve days. Going on thirteen now.

"It's concerning to think that the island might have been a pawn in Claudius's plot already back then." Favian shook his head and pushed away from the column. His peaceful island had managed to stay out of most of the fae machinations and politics over the years. But no longer.

"There is something stirring in the Realm of Monsters." Captain Antonio also straightened, taking a step forward. "I doubt this is the last time a peaceful court will find itself targeted."

A sobering thought. Favian would need to prepare his island better so that when the next attack came, they would be ready.

Favian released a long, slow breath. Despite the carnage in the streets and the night of fighting, he was more at peace than he had been for the past two years.

Chapter Nineteen

Viola glanced back at where Favian leaned against a column, facing Captain Antonio. While she was curious about the tale the human captain would tell, this was a conversation Favian needed to have in private. Hopefully he would trust her enough to tell her what was said.

Would he trust her? They were now bargained to marry, but that didn't mean he had forgiven her for the glamour and the lies and the half-truths she'd told in the past twelve days.

Something to worry about in the morning.

She turned away and pushed the door to the outpost open.

As soon as she stepped inside, she was confronted by two bookwyrms. They had their ruffs out, mouths hanging open to show their teeth.

When their slitted gazes focused on her, their ruffs went down and the snarls turned into something almost like grins as they slithered forward, giving their growling purrs.

After closing the door behind her, she bent and scratched them. "Belch. Toby. I'm glad to see you two survived the night all right."

"Viola?" Sebastian stepped from around the corner of the nearest bookshelf, his sword in his hand. "Are you all right? How is the island?"

"I'm fine. Favian and his guards fought off the rogue fae and the monsters." Viola urged her aching legs forward. All she wanted to do was collapse into bed. Well, wash off all the ick, then collapse into bed. "How are Olivia and the outpost? Did any monsters get in here?"

"We had to fight off a few of them. A rogue fae tried to rescue Lord Chauvlyn, but he didn't succeed." Sebastian grimaced, glancing down at his sword. Then he jabbed a finger over his shoulder. "We have him secured back there."

Viola nodded and set out in that direction, Sebastian falling into step at her side.

Around her, the outpost library thrummed with life. Branches grew out of the shelves, moving as they checked on the books. Flowering vines draped all the surfaces while more flowers sprouted from the new moss and grass growing between the paving stones.

She drew in a deep breath, then released it. The outpost was no longer a dead building. It was alive. It was home.

She blinked and shot a glance at Sebastian. "What's happening back home? Do you know? Lord Chauvlyn said our court is at war."

"He wasn't lying. Twelve days ago, the Court of Revels attacked the Court of Knowledge." Sebastian strode around the end of the shelves into the center of the outpost.

Viola followed, then caught her breath.

A large tree now filled the space, its branches reaching

over the shelves and spreading along the ceiling where they would keep the sunlight from damaging the precious books below.

Lord Chauvlyn sat with his back to the tree, bound with roots. Feste and Curio curled on the ground in front of Lord Chauvlyn's boots, eyeing him as if ready to start gnawing on him again if he so much as twitched the wrong way. Olivia stood beside him, holding Lord Chauvlyn's rapier.

Sebastian glared at Lord Chauvlyn. "King Theseus, Queen Hippolyta, and the swordmaidens have been holding them off. But the Great Library has had to suspend services, and life has become rather more dangerous than it has been previously."

Lord Chauvlyn just eyed him in return, his expression strangely blank now that he'd been defeated.

Beatrice. Meg. The children. Viola gritted her teeth and clenched her fists. Her nieces should have the chance to grow up in peace and safety—well, as much safety as generally could be expected in the Fae Realm. The Court of Knowledge was supposed to be a sanctuary, not a war zone.

Tonight, she had seen far too much death and destruction. So much pain unleashed on an innocent island. All because of Lord Chauvlyn and his king. Both of his kings.

Fae like Lord Chauvlyn—just like the evil humans back in the Human Realm—set out to destroy that peace and safety.

Why would he do stuff like this? Was he so evil that he lacked a heart? A soul? How could he look into the faces of the fae children and still hate so much that he could do something like this?

It wasn't right. Not at all.

Viola marched over to Lord Chauvlyn and glared down at him. "How can you be so cruel? Can you even love? Do you love? Or are you so heartless that you don't have a single person who you care about?"

Lord Chauvlyn's face twisted with something almost like pain before he returned to that blank resignation.

But it was enough.

"You think you love someone?" Viola jabbed him in the chest. She found herself gripping the glamour pendant with her other hand. It had become something of a comfort item to fiddle with in the past few days. "How can you do stuff like this and claim to love someone? Love doesn't work like that. Love is self-sacrificial. Kind. Loving. Not cruel and manipulative."

Lord Chauvlyn snorted. "And you are just naïve."

"Really?" Viola jabbed him in the chest with her finger again. "I've heard how my sister let you go and spared your life. And yet you still claim I don't know what I'm talking about. If you had family, you'd know what love was."

There was that twisting expression again. That hint of some deep emotion.

Who could Lord Chauvlyn possibly love? It didn't make sense that this evil fae lord could have a scrap of that emotion left in him.

She hadn't even consciously willed it but the shivery clinging glamour spread over her. She couldn't see much of herself besides dark trousers, slim hands, a boyish figure.

Lord Chauvlyn's face drained of color. His hands were bound behind his back, but he lunged at her anyway, straining against the roots. "Don't you dare wear his face!"

Viola staggered back and dropped the pendant. The

glamour vanished. Who had that been? Lord Chauvlyn's son? Brother?

Brother, most likely. His expression hadn't been paternal. More the same pain she'd carried around for nearly two weeks while Sebastian had been missing.

"That's enough of that." Sebastian shoved Lord Chauvlyn back against the tree. The roots tightened around him, pinning the fae lord in place. The two bookwyrms snarled, prepared to strike. Olivia tensed, the sword's tip swinging closer to Lord Chauvlyn's neck.

Lord Chauvlyn slumped against the tree, not resisting. His chin dipped low, something about the set of his shoulders more defeated and shattered than he had been a moment ago.

Viola straightened. She hadn't expected that to rattle him so much. She'd have to pass along what she had learned to Brigid. Her sister would be able to figure out how to best use that information.

When Lord Chauvlyn didn't make another move, Sebastian let him go and stepped back. He met Olivia's gaze, giving a slight nod.

Olivia, too, stepped back, and she lowered the sword.

Sebastian gestured. "Let's find somewhere more comfortable where we can talk. The bookwyrms will keep an eye on our prisoner."

The two bookwyrms gave matching snarls. Curio went so far as to snap at Lord Chauvlyn's boot. Lord Chauvlyn grimaced and drew his feet back.

Lord Chauvlyn would be well guarded, indeed.

Viola led the way through the bookshelves to one of the reading nooks. Perhaps a nook beside a window wasn't the safest place if there was a monster or two roaming the island yet, but it was comfortable and out of earshot of Lord Chauvlyn. With the tree now grown and the outpost an official extension of the Great Library, they would be well defended here.

Sebastian and Olivia settled on one side of the nook, setting their swords next to them so the weapons would be near to hand. Sebastian tucked his arm around Olivia's shoulders, the gesture comfortable.

The sight sent a pang through Viola. Sebastian and Olivia truly loved each other. They were comfortable in each other's presence, looking to each other for support on a difficult day.

That was what Viola wanted. Comfort. Support. The smiles and laughter.

Walks along the beach. Searching for shells. Discussing poetry in a library nook.

Ugh. She had it bad.

Olivia met Viola's gaze. "That was really you these past few days? The whole time?"

"Yes. I'm sorry I didn't just tell you. I wasn't sure what to do." Viola fake-glared at Sebastian. "*Someone* didn't tell us about you. Any of us. I didn't even know he had someone he cared about that way until that first day Favian—Duke Orsino—sent me to your manor with a message."

"I wanted to tell you. I would have told you, if things hadn't gone wrong." Sebastian's arm tightened around Olivia's shoulders as the two of them shared a look. "We were trying to keep it quiet. We didn't want Duke Orsino to find out by accident. Nor did we want to accidentally break the bargain."

Which they had done anyway, but Viola wasn't going to bring that up now. Instead, she kept her smile on her face, a light tone to her voice. "I understand. But it still made things awkward."

Olivia's mouth curved in the first hint of a smile. "I can imagine, especially that first day when you showed up and I threw myself at you."

Sebastian gave a smothered snort of a laugh.

"It was. A bit." Viola matched Olivia's smile, relaxing in the understanding she saw in Olivia's eyes. "If you'd touched me, you would've seen beneath the glamour. I was terrified you'd try to hug me. Or worse. Try to kiss me."

Sebastian's laugh turned into a choking sound. He coughed.

"Wouldn't that have been awkward." Olivia giggled, patting Sebastian's back. "I understand why you didn't tell me. There were plenty of secrets to go around."

"Yes, there were." Viola gave an exaggerated shudder. It had been bad. Hopefully things would be better, with everything out in the open.

Olivia leaned forward. "Sisters?"

"Sisters." Viola shared a smile with her new sister-in-law.

"I'm so glad to finally truly meet you. Sebastian has told me so much about your whole family. A big family with lots of sisters sounds so nice. All I had growing up was Favian, and he..." Olivia shrugged. "Well, with the tension of the last two years, he hasn't felt much like a friend or a brother. I'm hoping things can go back to the way they were, now that I'm not a part of the bargain."

Olivia trailed off, as if she just realized that she was only free of the bargain because Viola was now stuck in it instead.

Sebastian's jaw worked, his eyes flashing at the mention of the bargain.

Viola fiddled with the pendant of the glamour necklace, speaking before he had a chance to get huffy about the bargain again. "I hope so. You and Favian need each other as siblings."

Olivia smiled, the expression a touch sad, as she nodded.

"Speaking of siblings…" Sebastian pointed at the necklace. "I take it Brigid gave you that."

"Yes. Brigid gave it to me right before we left." Viola touched it, then let it fall back onto her blouse. "It got a little confusing, swapping back and forth between myself and you."

"You must have done a good job since no one figured it out." Sebastian grinned, then rested a hand on Olivia's shoulder. "And thank you for doing your best to protect Olivia."

"Even if it didn't turn out so well." Viola winced. She hadn't meant to make Olivia and Sebastian break the bargain. Granted, it wasn't fully on her. The two of them had known better, especially Sebastian, and they'd decided to get married anyway. But Viola still couldn't help but feel a tad guilty about that. "What happened to you after we were separated?"

Sebastian grimaced, looking away from both her and Olivia. "I was stuck between the realms for a week before Brigid, Munch, and Buddy found me and brought me home. That's when I found out the Court of Revels had attacked our court. Everyone is safe. The House, the Library, and Buddy are protecting them. They've been a bit harried, but King Theseus and Queen Hippolyta are holding their own.

It isn't like King Oberon or Queen Titania are all that bright when it comes to strategy and tactics."

"No. What tactics they have are probably provided by Claudius." Viola toyed with the edge of her skirt. She wasn't too worried about Munch and Brigid. They could take care of themselves.

But Basil and Meg? Their children? Beatrice? Basil and Meg could defend themselves if backed into a corner, and they would come out swinging if their girls were threatened. But Basil was a soft-spoken librarian at heart. And all Meg wanted to do was provide a safe place for her family.

They'd enjoyed seven years of relative peace in the Fae Realm. Yet it seemed that trouble had found them anyway.

"Hopefully Claudius will withdraw his support now that his plans to damage the Great Library and take over an island to use as a base in the Fae Realm have been thwarted." Sebastian rubbed the back of Olivia's hand with a thumb. "King Oberon won't stand a chance on his own."

Hopefully Sebastian was right. The Court of Knowledge was still home, even though Viola now had a new home here on Melyria.

"Well, if Claudius decides to attack again, we will be ready." Olivia rested her hand on the hilt of the sword she'd taken from Lord Chauvlyn.

Viola pulled the rapier she had been given by Lord Chauvlyn out of her pocket. She held it up. "I don't really know how to use this."

Olivia held up Lord Chauvlyn's other rapier, grinning. "I don't know how to use this either."

Yes, Viola was going to like having Olivia for a sister.

Chapter Twenty

Favian faced the Anywhere Door in the side garden. Viola stood beside him, the backs of their fingers nearly but never quite brushing. Should he take her hand? Did she want him to? How was he to know?

Facing him, Sebastian and Olivia held hands as they glanced between Favian and the Anywhere Door.

Favian reached into his pocket and drew out a folded message. "Librarian Sebastian, please give this to your King Theseus. It is an offer of sanctuary on the Island of Melyria for any noncombatants in his court who wish to flee the fighting. As a neutral court, it is within my power to make this offer, even if I can't help more."

"It is more than enough. Thank you, Duke Orsino." Sebastian took the message and tucked it into a pocket.

It didn't feel like enough, now that he'd seen the kind of death Claudius and his ilk could unleash on a court.

But Favian's island was already weakened. He didn't have anyone to spare to help King Theseus with the fighting. Hopefully offering sanctuary was helpful and wouldn't bring down more trouble on his island.

Sebastian turned to the Anywhere Door, Olivia at his side. He pulled her into his arms, speaking to her in a low tone.

With the outpost library now established, the Anywhere Door should work for the librarians. Theoretically. They wouldn't know until Sebastian tried the latch.

While Olivia was now a part of the Court of Knowledge, she wasn't an official librarian. As it was doubtful the Anywhere Door would let her through, she was staying here to look after the library while Sebastian and Viola were gone.

Favian glanced at Viola, then nodded toward the Door. "I'll watch over the outpost library until you get back."

It wasn't what he wanted to say. But now wasn't the time to speak his heart.

"I won't be gone long." Viola glanced between him and the Anywhere Door, opening her mouth as if she wanted to say something else. After a moment, she turned and hurried to Sebastian's side.

Olivia stepped away from Sebastian, joining Favian. He gave her a slight nod before the two of them faced the Anywhere Door.

Sebastian's shoulders rose and fell. Then he placed a hand on the Anywhere Door's latch and tugged.

For the first time in thirteen days, the Anywhere Door opened, giving a glimpse of a white marbled hall.

Sharing a glance with each other, Viola and Sebastian stepped through. The Anywhere Door swung shut behind them.

"They will be all right. They won't get stuck between the

realms this time." Favian clasped his hands behind his back, trying to tell himself that his words were true. It had been harder than he'd thought to watch Viola walk away.

But he wasn't even a member of the Court of Knowledge the way Olivia now was. There was no chance the Anywhere Door would allow him through during the current situation with the war.

"I know." Olivia released a shuddering breath before she turned more fully to him. "Favian, I am truly sorry for how everything went down. I never meant to hurt you, and I certainly never wanted to harm our island."

Favian sighed and nodded. "I'm sorry too for how I didn't listen to you. If I had, perhaps we could have figured out something together before it got to this point."

Olivia nodded, swallowing and blinking. "Do you think things can go back to the way they were? Between us?"

"No." Favian turned to her, wincing at the way her face fell. "We were children, Olivia. I don't think we can ever go back to that innocence. But perhaps we can move on, and things will be better than they were. After all, you are married to Sebastian. When I marry Viola, we will actually be brother and sister like we used to pretend."

"We will, won't we?" The soft smile returned to Olivia's face, and he knew the smile was more for Sebastian than for him. Then her gaze sharpened again, and she searched Favian's face. "You said *when*. You're going to marry Viola?"

"I certainly hope so." Favian felt a smile tug his own mouth.

VIOLA SAT in the dry sand, the waves washing up the beach, halting a foot or so away from her toes. The late afternoon sun beamed hot against the back of her neck, but she had no desire to move.

The squeaking of sand warned her of his approach a moment before Favian sat down next to her, barefoot and lacking a coat. His white shirt flapped in the slight breeze. His hair was still a bit damp, and he must have finally taken the time to wash up in the time she'd been gone visiting her family.

"How is everyone? Your guards? Your servants?" Viola swallowed, not wanting to ask her real question out loud.

Favian heaved a sigh and ran a hand through his hair, further tousling his damp hair. "There were a great number of grievous injuries among my guards and the villagers, but the healers are optimistic that they should pull through. Only three guards were killed. I am thankful it wasn't more, but it is still three too many. I suspect Claudius's army was waiting for the bulk of the monsters to go through first to cause chaos before the main invasion force came through. We must have closed the rifts just in time to prevent that from happening."

Viola opened her mouth, then closed it. What could she say? She certainly wasn't going to say something trite like *Could have been worse* or *I'm so sorry*. There really wasn't anything to say to something like last night.

Especially since a bunch of it was her family's fault. She had accidentally encouraged Sebastian and Olivia to break the bargain and cause the rifts. Claudius only focused on the island because the sapling was a way to weaken the Court of Knowledge.

She finally managed, "I'm glad the wounded are doing well."

"Yes." Favian leaned his elbows on his knees, his bare toes buried in the sand. "Two years ago, I thought burying my father was going to be my hardest day as the duke of Melyria. But last night—and, well, today—comes close."

"I'm sorry." Viola reached for him, but she stopped short of resting her hand on his arm. After a moment, she dropped her hand back to the sand, letting silence fall between them.

"How was your visit with your family?" Favian only flicked a glance at her before focusing once again on the crashing waves before them.

"Good. They survived the night of the attack all right." Viola dug a small pebble from the sand, then tossed it into the waves. It was too small to even make a plop, but the throwing motion released some of her tension. "Meg, Beatrice, and my nieces are probably going to be taking you up on your offer of sanctuary. Meg doesn't like leaving Basil alone to keep defending the Library, but they both want the girls to be safe."

"While I'm grieved at the reason for their visit, they are welcome to stay as long as they need." Favian rubbed a pebble between his fingers before he, too, tossed it into the waves. "I look forward to meeting your family. Some of them, anyway."

"I can't wait for you to meet them." Viola wiggled her toes in the sand. Was it wrong to feel guilty that she was enjoying the peace of this island while her family remained in danger?

Even though she had just visited, she still missed her family and missed the Court of Knowledge. But this island had wrapped itself around her heart in a way she hadn't expected it would when she arrived thirteen days ago.

It wasn't just the island that had a hold of her. The fae duke beside her also claimed a large chunk of her heart.

Despite the tension crackling between them, the soothing sound of the crashing waves and the warmth of the sun relaxed her muscles.

After several long moments, Favian reached into a pocket and drew out a folded piece of paper. He held it out to her. "It isn't finished, and it isn't very good. But, well, it's for you."

His eyes were such a deep liquid brown that for a moment, she couldn't tear her gaze away long enough to take the paper. But she shook herself, grabbed the paper, and unfolded it.

Her stomach sank. She recognized the first couple of lines. This was the poem she'd helped him start for Olivia.

Except the hair color was wrong. Blonde instead of Olivia's black curls. Blue eyes instead of brown.

He could have just changed it in the past few hours since Viola had become a substitute in the bargain.

But that would have messed up the rhyme scheme, clumsy as the rhyming was. He would have had to re-write whole portions of it to make it work, and based on the deep hollows beneath his eyes, he hadn't gotten any sleep and wasn't in any shape for revising poetry.

Then there were the lines about the walk along the beach and the library nook. Those could only have been about Viola.

She lowered the page and gaped at him. "When did you write this?"

"Over the past few days." His smile curved slightly

lopsided, though something in his eyes remained slightly sad. "I tried to write it about Olivia but I just…couldn't. At the time, I knew it was wrong when I was still in the bargain to marry Olivia, but I couldn't help but write it about you. I intended to burn it."

"I'm glad you didn't." Viola smoothed the paper over her knees, her heart beating with a strange rhythm in her chest.

"I think we have something between us. Maybe not love yet. But I…like…you." Favian's gaze dropped to the sand to focus on his toes.

How was it possible that his bare feet could make her stomach give such fluttery flips? Or maybe it was his stilted words.

She unstuck her dry tongue from the roof of her mouth. "I like you too."

He huffed out a breath, still not looking at her. "Olivia and I liked each other too. Not in a romantic way. But we were close. Then the bargain ruined that. I don't want that to happen to us. I don't want you to resent me or feel forced or anything. But, Viola." He finally looked at her, turning to more fully face her. "This time, I'm bargaining for who *I* want to marry. But if you don't want to marry me, we can find another substitute. I can't get out of it, but you can."

Did she want out of this bargain? A part of her didn't want to be forced. She'd said yes mostly to close the rifts.

Yet whenever she thought about trying to find a substitute, thinking about Favian bound to marry someone else, her stomach went from fluttering to churning. She'd spent much of the last twelve days jealous of Olivia because she was the one Favian was supposed to marry.

"I think you're stuck with me." Viola worked up the

courage to smile. "After all, I only have one unmarried sister left, and she's not even eighteen yet. Way too young."

"Are you sure? I don't want—" Favian began, but Viola pressed a finger to his mouth.

"Yes, I'm sure. Who else is going to write me terrible poetry or discuss various organizational methods." Even as she said it, her own certainty sank deep into her bones. Maybe she didn't want to marry him tomorrow, but she wanted the freedom to get to know him better and keep falling in love. The only way to do that was to agree to the bargain.

Favian reached up and clasped her hand, pulling it away from his mouth. As soon as their fingers touched, a soft glow surrounded their hands.

Viola stared, first at their hands, then up at him, then down at their hands again.

Favian, too, gaped down at their fingers. "Huh." He dragged his gaze up to meet hers. "This never happened with Olivia. I thought it was because the bargain wasn't enough to start a binding, but…"

"Clearly that isn't the case." Viola resisted the urge to pull away. Not that she minded holding Favian's hand. It was just strange to see her hand glow.

"No." Favian turned their hands over, as if examining the glow from all sides to make research notes. "Perhaps because Olivia wasn't willing. I wasn't either, though I convinced myself I was."

"That could be it." Viola linked her fingers with his rather than let go. This was further confirmation that she'd made the right choice. They were in this bargain together. Except…she couldn't help but grimace. "Does this mean we have to get married right away? I like you, but I don't really want to marry you right this minute. I'd rather take time courting first. But I know how dangerous it is to leave bindings half done."

"In the normal course of things, yes." Favian's resting frown face returned as he regarded their hands. "But this binding is from a bargain. Unlike being snatched, this binding can't be turned into something else. It has to end in our marriage since the wording of the bargain is clear on that. As long as we are clear in our intentions to keep the bargain, we are in no danger by leaving it unfinished for a while."

"Oh, good." Viola released a breath, her shoulders relaxing.

Favian's eyebrows rose. "Should I be offended that you sound so happy about that?"

"Nope, not at all." She shifted a bit closer, pretending she didn't feel the way sand was working its way into her skirts. The beach was lovely, but sand had a bad habit of getting everywhere. "I think I'm going to really like getting to know you better."

"I just have one request." Favian gestured with his free hand to the necklace still hanging around her neck. "Please. No more glamours."

"No more glamours." Viola gripped the pendant with her free hand. Though, she was reluctant to take it off. "Or perhaps we should come up with a code word so we know we are ourselves and not someone in a glamour."

"A wise precaution." Favian's mouth curved into a wry twist. "I want to make sure it's actually you I'm getting to know."

"Yes, it would be awkward to enjoy certain moments with anyone else." Viola dropped the necklace's pendant.

For this moment, she was fully herself. "Like walks along the beach. Horrible poetry."

"Long discussions about random topics while we're sitting in one of the nooks in the outpost library." Favian leaned closer as he gently swept a strand of her hair behind her ear. His hand lingered, his fingers brushing her cheek.

"How about snuggling in a library nook?" Viola found herself swaying closer.

"While your brother is there? I don't believe that would be conducive to my health."

"He has Olivia. I'll just ask her to keep him occupied." As soon as she said it, she almost wished she hadn't. A flash of something flickered through Favian's eyes. Pain. Regret. "Sorry. I probably shouldn't have brought her up."

"No, it's all right. Just…strange." Favian traced her cheek with his thumb. "I've spent years thinking I was going to marry her. Yet she was a friend and a sister before that."

"And now she will be your sister, once we're married." Perhaps it was best to talk about this now. After Viola's brother had gone behind Favian's back in courting Olivia, it was better to have everything in the open now.

"That's somehow less strange." Favian shook his head, giving a breath of a laugh. His laughter died as his thumb brushed Viola's lower lip. "I never kissed her."

"All right." Viola drew out the word, not sure why he was telling her this. Her skin was starting to flush hot, though that could have been the sun. Or her thought that she would rather have him kiss her than talk about kissing. Especially kissing Olivia.

"It just seems important for you to know." Favian's voice softened, almost a whisper, as he leaned a bit closer. But he didn't close the last few inches, just kept cradling her face, tracing his thumb gently over her skin, sending tingles down her spine.

"Thanks for telling me." Talking was the last thing on Viola's mind. If only Favian would hurry up and kiss her.

But he seemed to be waiting for something. A sign from her, perhaps.

She wasn't sure what sign to give him. Her head was feeling a bit light. Her stomach fluttering. Her heart hammering. She was either going to be ill or she was falling in love. One of the two.

"Of course." Favian murmured the words as he brushed his thumb over her chin. Then, finally, he kissed her.

Viola kissed him back, wrapping her fingers in the warmth of his shirt to tug him closer.

Yep, definitely falling in love. If she hadn't already been in a bargain to marry him, she would have bargained to do just that, no matter how risky it was to make a bargain with the fae. Because this risk—the risk of her heart, of falling in love—was worth it with him.

<h1 style="text-align:center">Epilogue</h1>

ONE YEAR LATER...

Favian strolled down the dock, thankful to be done with paperwork for the day. He'd left his coat back in the study, and the sea breezes tugged at his loose, white shirt.

As he approached the end of the dock, there was a splash. Viola turned around, a notebook and a pen clutched in her hand. "I just finished talking with a siren about siren tears. It was so fascinating. I can't wait to write this all down and add it to the library. It turns out, sea glass is created by any siren tears, but the emotion behind the tears affects the color. Blues and greens are the most common colors, and those are sad colors. It's sad to think that the most common siren tears are sad ones."

"Yes." Favian sat on the end of the dock next to her, letting his legs dangle over the water.

"But it means the one I found on that first walk along the beach was a happy tear." Viola dug into her pocket and pulled out the opaque pink sea glass. "This one was shed in joy, likely some kind of joy of love."

"Fitting." Favian clasped his hand over hers, rubbing his thumb over the back of her hand. Even a year later, their hands still glowed, a testament to the binding that had only grown stronger between them.

"Yes." She leaned her head against his shoulder, snuggling closer.

He wrapped an arm around her shoulders. This was it. The moment he'd been waiting for. Nothing could be more right than this.

He reached into his pocket and pulled out a piece of paper. "I have something for you."

His heart pounded in his throat, but he refused to look away. Whatever her reaction, he wanted to watch every nuance flash across her face a moment before her answer either unraveled him or knit him back together in all the best ways possible.

VIOLA BLINKED at Favian's all-too-earnest expression before she took the paper and unfolded it, revealing a short poem.

The beach is white.
The ocean is blue.
I don't know if you know,
But I love you.

THE PALACE IS WHITE.
The bookwyrms are blue.
Will you marry me?

I'd like to marry you.

Viola laughed and shook her head, not sure if she should cringe at the terrible poetry or kiss him for being so sweet.

When she glanced up, she found he was holding a long blue ribbon.

"Yes!" Viola snatched the ribbon out of his hand. "Yes, I'll marry you. Yes, I love you too. Just…yes."

Cringe at the poetry or kiss him?

Definitely kiss him.

Free Ebook!

Thanks so much for reading *Night of Secrets*! I hope you enjoyed the cozy romance between Favian and Viola! If you loved the book, please consider leaving a review on Amazon or Goodreads. Reviews help your fellow readers find books that they will love.

If you ever find typos in my books, feel free to message me on social media or send me an email through the Contact Me page of my website.

If you want to learn about all my upcoming releases, get great book recommendations, and see a behind-the-scenes glimpse into the writing process, join my newsletter at www.taragrayce.com.

Did you know that if you sign up for my newsletter, you'll receive lots of free goodies? You will receive the free novella *Steal a Swordmaiden's Heart*, which is set in the same world as *Stolen Midsummer Bride* and *Bluebeard and the Outlaw*! This novella is a prequel to *Stolen Midsummer Bride,* and tells the story of how King Theseus of the Court of Knowledge won the hand of Hippolyta, Queen of the Swordmaidens.

If you don't wish to sign up for my newsletter, *Steal a*

Swordmaiden's Heart is available on Amazon, though it isn't in KU like the rest of the series.

You will also receive the free novella *Torn Curtains*, a fantasy Regency Beauty and the Beast retelling. This one isn't available anywhere else besides my newsletter!

Sign up for my newsletter now

Don't Miss the Next Adventure

Dance of Nothing

Fated mates...with her childhood nemesis.

From the moment Beatrice found a home in the Court of Knowledge, Benedict, the arrogant son of a fae lord, has been her nemesis.

Benedict has spent the past year as a prisoner. Upon regaining his freedom, he returns to the Court of Knowledge with a new perspective and the desire to repair past relationships. Too bad it is just too easy and too much fun to ruffle Beatrice's feathers.

When a Midsummer Revel brings them together and reveals that they are fated mates, Beatrice is determined to find a way out of the binding, no matter what it takes. Even if Benedict is determined to change her mind.

As misunderstandings abound, will these fated mates fall in love or will their history tear them apart forever?

This loose retelling of Shakespeare's *Much Ado About Nothing* is tentatively coming 2026!

Acknowledgments

After so many books, it is becoming harder and harder to thank everyone in new and creative ways! You are all so supportive and encouraging and I couldn't do this writing thing without each and every one of you!

To my readers: Thank you for picking up my books and investing time and money into my stories! I'm so honored whenever you read my book out of all of the millions of books out there!

To my parents: I wouldn't be where I am today if you hadn't encouraged my dreams. You always made me feel like I could do anything, and I wouldn't be the writer I am today without that fearlessness to face challenges you gave me.

To my siblings (both my brothers and my sisters-in-law): If I have cute romances in my books, it is because all of you provide inspiration for what that looks like!

To my friends (Bri, Paula, and Jill): For all the hugs and girl trips and laughter over the years! Very few people are blessed with a close group of friends-for-life as seen in books and movies, and I'm beyond grateful to be one of the few!

To my writer friends (Molly, Morgan, Addy, Savannah, Sierra, Liz, Victoria, Kristen, Anna, and so many others): I don't know what I'd do without the brainstorming, the commiseration, the encouragement, the texts, the emails, the squee moments, and all the rest!

To my writer group (Steve, Mike, Kim, Brad, Bri, Dylan, McKenna, Michelle, Liz, and Ashley): I look forward each month to a night of laughter and tangents!

To my proofreaders (Mindy and Deborah): Thanks so much for going through this book and polishing up all the typos and errors before they became too embarrassing! And for laughing over my Princess Bride references and fangirling over my characters with me!

COURT OF MIDSUMMER MAYHEM

Stolen Midsummer Bride

Steal a Swordmaiden's Heart

Forest of Scarlet

Wild Fae Primrose

Night of Secrets

A VILLAIN'S EVER AFTER

Bluebeard and the Outlaw

SACRIFICED HEARTS

Mountain of Dragons and Sacrifice

Of Dragons and Stone

TETHERED HEARTS

Ties of Bargains

<u>Middle Grade</u>

PRINCESS BY NIGHT

Lost in Averell

www.ingramcontent.com/pod-product-compliance
Lightning Source LLC
Chambersburg PA
CBHW070626170726
48291CB00003B/900